MW00928489

MEADOWLARK

MEADOWLARK

JOYCE MARGARET HUFF

Library of Congress Control Number: 2018905062
ISBN: Hardcover   978-1-9845-2422-5
                 Softcover   978-1-9845-2421-8
                 eBook   978-1-9845-2420-1

This is a work of fiction. All of the characters, names, incidents, organizations, and dialogue in this novel are either the products of the author's imagination or are used fictitiously.

Cover Photo by Terry L. Sohl http://sdakotabirds.com

Print information available on the last page.

Rev. date: 04/25/2018

To order additional copies of this book, contact:
Xlibris
1-888-795-4274
www.Xlibris.com
Orders@Xlibris.com
778610

This book is dedicated to my grandmother,

Margaret Elizabeth Christie Saunders
December 26, 1902 – October 12, 1996

PROLOGUE

Nebraska means "broad water" or "flat river", called Nebrathka by the Otos Indians who roamed the prairie land, hunting and raising children, long before the white man arrived. Located in the heart of America, its people were of pioneer stock, having endured the hardships of cold winters, floods and tornadoes as they farmed the land and buried children. The old Nebraskan saying "where the west begins" unabashedly points out that nothing of any significance happens in the state, that it was just an entryway to where real life began -- a foyer in a large mansion -- while everyone was glad the foyer was there, no time was spent in it. Like the modesty of the unassuming Nebraskan himself, it states the obvious without shame.

The local New Jersey newspaper carried a shocking headline: a township woman killed herself that week. She had thrown herself in front of a train going sixty miles an hour. The article went on to say she left a husband and two children. She was forty-six years old.

Julia read the story but was not outraged as were her neighbors. She did not think LeeAnn Doane was selfish, as her friends believed. She had known this woman, though not well. The speculation as to why she killed herself went on for months. Some townspeople hinted she was bored; some said she was a secret drinker; many believed she was just painfully lonely. To look at her, no one could have predicted that she would ever do such a thing. One evening she was sitting at a PTA meeting, smiling, the following week she was being cleaned off a track by the fire department.

LeeAnn Doane died in late October. Her obituary stated she was a New Jersey woman who had been born and raised in Nebraska. Several weeks before hearing of the death, Julia had received an email. Before the email came, she would not have been able to comprehend what made LeeAnn so unhappy that she knelt down in front of the 5:37 A.M. train. But now she could understand and with that understanding came empathy.

It was strange but when life gets busy, a person does not often reflect on the past. The years have a way of slipping by unnoticed. Julia had nearly forgotten who she was during the years of mothering her four children. Now forty-five years old, life was settling into a quiet routine. Her children had grown into adolescents and needed her less. Time was more her own.

Then came the email – Nebraska -- and with it, a flood of memories.

She put her head down against the keyboard and wept. She had not cried years ago when she had first heard what had happened but she cried now. She cried off and on for an entire week, her tears dripping on the morning newspaper, in the car, on the sliced bologna she put in her children's sandwiches. Her husband would walk by, shaking his head, her children wondering amongst themselves if menopause were setting in.

LeeAnn Doane had not yet thrown herself on the track. Julia would shed no tears for her although she pitied her despair. It was the memory of another death that caused her mourning. And it too was such a lonely way to die.

CHAPTER ONE

The little boy was only four but everyone said he was his mother's little man. Slight of build like Mother, he had his father's black hair and dark eyes. In fact, except for his small frame, he looked very much like his father. His mother was blond and fair and reminded the boy of a fairy princess from one of this books. He went everywhere with his mother and she always held his hand. It wasn't that she was overprotective; rather, she liked the feeling of closeness.

When Mother had to go somewhere without him, the little boy would weep in dejection until his father, a Midwestern farmer of broad girth, became disgusted. He'd whack his son with the back of his weathered hand and the child fell back, stunned into silence. "You're acting like a little girl," his father would mumble. He'd point to the boy's younger brother, Guenther, and say "You don't see him carrying on now, do you?" Guenther was a large boy, husky for three years of age, a child who rarely cried, sunny in nature even as a toddler. He had once fallen off a fence and split open his chin without a whimper. Guenther adored his father and sometimes to gain his attention, would turn against his older brother. "You're such a baby," Guenther would taunt if he caught his brother weeping. "Are you sure you're even a boy?"

Guenther's disappointment in having such a weak older brother did not bother him. The child only felt the sharp sting of being a total disappointment to his father.

"Hey, Julia," Jenny Murden said, plopping down next to her friend on a battered couch in the student lounge. "You won't believe this, but there's an English professor here who's just your type. I took one look at him and said 'an old guy and just her type'."

Jenny's twin, Laine, nodded. The year was 1974. The sisters, eighteen years old, had been Julia Jahns' best friends since junior high. Laine and Jenny were identical twins, finishing each other sentences and hard to tell apart.

They adored Julia whom they thought was prettier, nicer than both of them put together and easy to control. Yet many times they found her puzzling.

Together the three girls attended the local two year college, Raleigh, which was situated in the small northwest New Jersey town of Crane Ridge. Forty miles from New York City, Crane Ridge was a quiet, suburban borough with tree-lined streets and little shops that came alive mostly on weekends. Rich enough to have Belgian block curbing but too poor to be the desired abode of the wealthy, it was home to one movie theater, two diners, a family-run sandwich shop, several boutiques, an ice cream parlor, three churches (two Protestant and one Catholic), a Jewish temple and a youth center that was rarely utilized by any youth. For all its simplicity, the people of Crane Ridge were proud of their town, picturesque like a Norman Rockwell painting, with little crime, few juvenile delinquents and located far enough from the notorious turnpike to make them feel exempt from the butt of any New Jersey jokes. Unlike several other neighboring townships, it possessed no "rich" and "poor" sections so no one could claim they came from either the right or wrong side of the tracks. Most of the houses were built at the same time, post-World War II, on small lots, modest but not shabby. Lawns and gardens were kept up, people watched out for each other's children and there was little gossip. Very few married women worked outside the home and if they did, it was part-time. The few apartments in Crane Ridge were the ones created over the shops and housed either newlyweds or the newly divorced. And divorce was not a huge problem for Crane Ridge in the mid-1970s. If it happened, it was seen as a tragedy, the participants to be pitied.

It was this quiet setting in which Julia Jahns and her friends spent their time growing up. They had missed the wild sixties by a few years and were sheltered from anything going on in the early seventies by their church-going mothers.

During the summer of 1974, after high school graduation and before the three girls were to start classes at Raleigh College, Jenny and Laine Murden saved their money and bought a car. Like most things they owned, they shared it. When college began that September, they picked up Julia each morning and took her home when classes ended. Julia could not afford a vehicle so several days a week she waited around campus for her friends' classes to end to get a ride home. She spent her idle hours in the student lounge, doing homework or watching people pass by, not noticing her or even wondering why someone spent so many hours alone on an old gray couch. No one ever stopped to say hello or ask if she needed help. She was both comforted and horrified by her own invisibility.

The Murden girls and Julia were insecure young women who had banded together in 1969 as thirteen year olds, seeking solace in their shared misery. For they had endured more than the usual amount of teen-aged angst, having no father living at home, their outlook on life fringed with bleakness. They had gravitated toward each other in junior high as if prompted by an unseen force. Jenny swore it was God's hand, for the three girls were not only from divorced homes (a rarity in 1969) but very religious as well.

The girls first met in music class. Julia immediately admired the twins for their bold faith. She had observed the way they "witnessed" about Christ to their classmates, handing out tracts without any self-consciousness. For Julia also loved Christ and considered herself "born again" but lacked the nerve to speak out about it. The twins were able to convince Julia and her family to leave their Baptist Church and attend a Pentecostal one several towns away. The passionate fervor of the worship was attractive to both Julia and her mother. It was there that she felt peace and comfort, glad she was now at a place where she felt even closer to her God. She had also gained two best friends. And for a while, the friendship flourished.

Julia's mother and the twins' mother, having first met at St. John's Pentecostal Church, were surprised to discover they were both divorcees and both working as waitresses. An instant bond developed between the two thirty-something women even though they later learned the reasons for their divorces were not similar.

Jenny and Laine Murden lived with their mother in a one-bedroom apartment in the middle of Crane Ridge over a sandwich shop. Julia did not live far from them, sharing a petite A-frame house with her mother and two younger brothers. Many times the twins lamented the fact that Julia lived in a house with a backyard, enjoyed her own bedroom and was a big sister to two little brothers. Julia, in turn, envied the twins the intimacy of their twinship while wishing she too had a father who was as interested in her as Mr. Murden was in his daughters.

Chet Murden was tall, handsome and dashing, with flashing dark blue eyes and a thick mop of hair. He was only nineteen years older than his girls and a major presence in their lives. Julia's own father not only seemed disinterested in his children, but lived halfway across the country, rarely seen or heard from. His child support checks always arrived on time but his lack of communication stung.

Laine and Jenny were proud of their youthful father and delighted in reminding Julia of his devotion to them. As the years passed, the thorn that was Chet Murden grew larger in Julia's side. The twins took every opportunity to brag about their good-looking, athletic father who lived in the next town and often dropped by to visit them. However, inasmuch as Chet Murden called his twins "my beauties", to their chagrin, the two girls knew deep inside love was truly blind. For though they had inherited his height and dense, chestnut-colored hair, by genetic misfortune Jenny and Laine resembled their mother. Their beady pale green eyes were too closely spaced together, peeking out from under drooping eyelids. Large uneven white teeth crowded their small mouths. Their noses were bulbous in shape and did not seem the right size for their small, angular faces. They wore their coarse hair long and straight, as was the style of the day, parted in the middle. Tall in stature, they had athletic, large-boned frames.

Julia, in contrast, was more finely chiseled. Five feet five inches tall, she was slender with long legs. Many people found her attractive though she did little to enhance any God-given assets. Large, round blue eyes were hidden behind unbecoming glasses. She seldom used make-up. Fine, wispy hair, a shade between blond and light brown, hung limply around her face. Trying for years to grow it long, it had refused to cooperate, so she gave up and let it hang just to the end of her chin. She had a small straight nose and deep pink, bow-shaped lips, but her face was not symmetrical enough to be labeled "pretty". She had no cheekbones to speak of, but her skin was clear with invisible pores, like peaches and cream. "English skin" her grandmother had called it, a complexion the twins envied for they struggled with acne. No matter how often Laine and Jenny complimented her, Julia did not agree. She did not like her looks. When surrounded by a crowd, she felt as insignificant as a wren in a tree of cardinals.

Whenever life became stressful for Julia, she would cloister herself in her room and watch old home movies. Her mother was wise enough to leave her alone at such times. Ruth Jahns kept an old movie projector in Julia's bedroom. Canisters of sixteen millimeter film lay atop her bureau. There were hours' worth of film, most of it featuring Julia who had been the Jahnses' oldest child.

Since Julia began classes at Raleigh College, Ruth Jahns noticed an increase in her daughter's movie watching. Marge Coppins, her older sister, scolded her.

"Stop worrying so much, Ruthie. Starting college is a difficult time. If the movies give Julia comfort, then so be it. She's remembering a happier, quieter time. Better to relive her past than to be out drinking and carousing with dozens of young men and other ne'er-do-wells."

Ruth Jahns looked doubtful.

"Be glad she's a good kid," Marge said. "If this is the worst thing she does, you can praise God in that holy roller church of yours. This is 1974, not 1944. We lived in a far different time. Most girls these days sleep around with every young Casanova that strikes their fancy and what happens? You wind up a grandma, your kid drops out of school and works in the five and dime the rest of her life. These young fellas don't even want to marry the girls anymore!"

The subject of young men was pursued no further. Both Marge Coppins and Ruth Jahns knew that Julia had not yet expressed any interest in dating a young man. Unlike the twins, who were boy crazy, Julia had taken a liking to men much older than herself. Nothing ever came of these infatuations but her mother found it worrisome. It had begun when Julia was thirteen and had a crush on one of her teachers. The crush lasted three long years. Ruth Jahns fretted while Marge Coppins felt it was a phase her niece would soon outgrow.

"It's because Wes isn't here," Ruth Jahns would say, referring to her ex-husband and father of her children. "She goes for these men because Wes is gone."

"Men? I thought it was just that teacher," Marge said.

"That one's her obsession. But she liked the eye doctor, too," Ruth said. "He was forty-five. And the fellow who works at the bank. He's a little younger. But you're right. The teacher was the main one."

"Thank goodness none of the men she likes saw her as anything more than a child," Marge responded. "Let's hope it stays that way till she gets over all this."

Ruth sighed. Her daughter had been a happy and outgoing child until her twelfth year. After entering seventh grade, the first year of junior high, Ruth and Wesley Jahns had broken up. Wesley moved out west and remarried soon after. Why he left so suddenly stunned all who knew him. It hadn't been a love affair because he had never been the womanizing type. Ruth Jahns knew the fears that had eaten at her husband, one of them poverty. Wesley had grown up in an insecure home, his father sick and forever losing jobs. Many days Wes left for school without food in his stomach. He had let that fear stay with him into adulthood. He was offered a higher-paying job in North Dakota around the time Julia was entering sixth grade. Ruth Jahns did not want to move.

Wesley did not stick around to argue. He left. And he married a woman he met at his office not long afterward.

The months following his departure were lonely and frightening. Ruth Jahns juggled two part-time jobs, trying to hide her desperation from her children. Julia sensed the tension and became withdrawn. Her school work suffered and she daydreamed.

Looking at the world, once so full of color, Julia now only saw muted grays. She did not like being a teenager and she did not like her present life. Her father's absence had hit her harder than she had thought it ever would. She felt rejected and ugly. The one bright spot in her world was her junior high geography teacher whom she worshipped with a passion. He had consumed her thoughts. She focused on him like a starving entity focuses on a banquet table. There was nothing romantic about it. Her mother did not at all understand her love for him which she found annoying. The love was beyond description, like worship, yet far more delightful. She felt she could be in this man's presence with nothing ever happening, his nearness elevating her to the height of ecstasy. When he walked by her desk, she would inhale deeply, trying to capture his essence.

"He doesn't know you're alive," Jenny once told her.

"He certainly doesn't know you're in love with him," Laine added.

Not only did the twins not comprehend her feelings, her mother and aunt were puzzled as well.

"You don't want to have a date with him, do you?" her mother once asked, looking worried.

"I hope you don't plan on marrying him," Jenny had said. "You know that's impossible. First of all, he would have to wait for you to grow up. Then he'd have to divorce his wife. And maybe he won't divorce her. Because he had a kid with her."

"Don't you see his wedding band?" Laine added. "He wears it every day."

She would shake her head.

It's not that, she thought. *You two will never understand.* But she did not say the words out loud. How can you explain a mystical experience to someone who has never been enthralled? It was like explaining faith to an unbeliever.

"Yes, we know your type of man, Jules: middle-aged, thin with dark hair. I'd say this guy's about forty. Old!" Laine now said, emphasizing the word "old". "You've just got to sign up for his class next semester. He's somebody you'd go for. And he's a teacher!"

"If you do," Jenny added, "the three of us would be together. Laine and I already signed up for his eight a.m. class. For us, English lit is a requirement."

"Oh?" Julia responded, not lifting her eyes from her book. "He's probably married. Anyway, I've already signed up for Speech which I need to take. He teaches a course that is useless for my major."

"No, he's not married," Jenny said. "He's a bachelor. He says he lives in solitary bliss and besides, he comes to class with the hems of his pants held up with safety pins."

Julia turned to Jenny, her eyeglasses slipping down her nose. It was obvious the twins were remembering her three year adoration of Geography Teacher. Why else would they be mentioning this professor? Since junior high, they had taken notice of Julia's mini-crushes on an assortment of older men. They found it annoying that she had never been interested in boys her own age. This fact sometimes rankled them, depending on their mood. Being very much into young men of their generation, the twins could not comprehend Julia's obsession with "old people". They would pester her to change, to get a boyfriend, to group date with them. Julia's mother, in her daughter's defense, once told the twins Julia had a "father complex", a problem she was sure would disappear once her daughter had fully matured.

"Well, the next time we pass his classroom, I'll take a look at him," Julia said, dismissing their words. She was sure her friends were mistaken. A man in his forties who was still single? Impossible. She remembered Geography Teacher. He had been thirty-four and married and even had a child. Men never made it to their forties before taking a wife.

Several days passed by before Julia recalled their conversation. She and Laine were chatting in the hallway outside Laine's psychology class.

"So where is this Professor Hunter?" Julia asked.

"Oh, yeah, his room is right down the hall," Laine said. "Let's see if he's in there. We have to be quiet otherwise it will look weird. Peek in quick and see what you think. I swear to you, Jenny's right! He's just your type."

The classroom door was halfway open, the murmur of voices audible. Professor Hunter, forty-four years old, was in the in the middle of writing a sentence on the chalkboard. Julia looked at him, uttering an involuntary gasp, which he seemed to hear.

Aiden Hunter stood five feet, eight inches tall, with a small frame draped in clothes that hung unbecomingly. His hair was silky fine and jet black, and his dark brown eyes reminded her of two pools of muddy water. His skin was white without a touch of either olive or pink, giving him a waiflike appearance. His small face belied a sad expression, as if he were remembering a time when he had been happy but yet resigned as if he knew he could never be happy again. He had a small straight nose over lips that were so dark red in color they appear bruised. His lower lip jutted out further than his upper lip, giving him a petulant expression.

"He's your type," Laine whispered. "I have to go."

She left Julia standing there, staring at Aiden, who looked back at her, the chalk in his fingers.

CHAPTER TWO

In the winter of 1975 Julia Jahns felt like a brand new adult. Like most eighteen-going-on-nineteen year olds, she faced her life with hopeful anticipation and idealistic dreams. Paradoxically she often felt frightened and confused. Her days had fallen into a steady pattern of school, work and studies. Employed part-time at Roote's, she had little money in her pocket. She studied hard but her heart was not passionate about becoming a kindergarten teacher. Nonetheless she took courses to push herself in that direction. At the time Julia was not even sure she liked children. But this was the seventies, an era when most high school guidance counselors steered their B-student females into the field of education. It was either that or nursing. Julia was not strong in math and hated the thought of dealing with odorous human bodies, so being a teacher seemed the logical choice. Laine and Jenny decided to go into accounting, not only because they enjoyed numbers, but found it was a field full of available men.

Raleigh College was the two-year institution picked by both Mrs. Murden and Mrs. Jahns for their daughters' educations. It was cheap and close to home. Located on the perimeter of Crane Ridge, it was considered to be a glorified high school. Most of its students resided either in or near Crane Ridge, going home between classes. No one lived on campus. The passionate pursuit of a social life remained the main focus of most Raleigh students, making them no different than collegians everywhere. Enjoyment was obtained in the neighboring town bars, places to disco dance, drink and meet the opposite sex.

Julia's ideas on how to conduct herself socially differed from those of her friends. Though coaxed continuously, she refused to set foot in a bar to either drink or dance. A devout churchgoer, she felt such activities were for the weak of character. Sin, to her, was sin. Being a moralist and hating any kind of hypocrisy, she felt pressed to live up to her ideals. She was convinced

Laine and Jenny were discarding their godly roots by the enticement of what she termed the "fast lane".

"I don't think Pastor Griffith would approve of us going to those places," Julia said to the twins one afternoon in the student lounge. "Didn't you remember his sermon last Sunday about places we go? He said if you'd be embarrassed for Jesus to see you there, it's a place you shouldn't be going to at all."

Jenny had just informed her friends of her evening plans. Having spent the past weekend shopping, she donned a new polyester pantsuit which her friends had spent the past ten minutes admiring. Several of the girls' coworkers from the five-and-dime store, Roote's, also attended Raleigh. Between classes they would sit together in the student lounge. Two of them, Mary Lou Sipaski and Pammy Haus, were amiable but unattractive girls. They were fond of Julia but being weaker personalities, if a conflict arose in their chatter, they both felt it unwise to contradict the Murden twins. Julia would voice an opinion, Jenny and Laine would voice theirs, and if the consensus were mixed, Julia usually lost out.

Several evenings during the week, Mary Lou and Pammy would accompany the twins to the local watering holes. All four hoped to find boyfriends and if their mission failed, to give each other moral support. Julia never wanted to go with them but that did not deter Jenny from continuing to invite her.

"Yes, I heard Pastor's message," Jenny responded. "Pandora's is more like a dance place than a bar. And we're not actually going there to drink. My mother always said dancing isn't really that much of a sin. Besides, I'm sick of sitting home every night. How are we supposed to meet guys? There's no one exciting at this school. And there's absolutely no one in church. I'm tired of being by myself. It's depressing."

"You'll never meet a boyfriend sitting in the student lounge, Jules," Laine said. "Or staying home reading every night."

Julia felt like pointing out that Laine and Jenny had not met anyone by bar hopping but she kept quiet.

"I don't want to be an old maid," Jenny pouted. "If I'm not married by age twenty-five I think I'll kill myself."

"Don't you want to eventually meet someone?" Laine pressed, looking at Julia. "They don't just walk into your living room."

"Oh, Julia will meet someone someday," said Mary Lou. "My mom always told me for every lid, there's a pot. Or is it for every pot there's a lid?"

"Except Julia likes all the cracked pots!"

The girls laughed at Jenny's remark.

"If you try to find a guy here at Raleigh, you'll definitely end up an old maid," Pammy said. "An eternal virgin!" She looked around. "There's nobody I'd want to go out with at this place."

"Stay a virgin forever?" Jenny said. "That's a fate worse than death. It's worse than getting cancer!"

There was a pause as everyone considered a lifetime of singleness.

"To think some women do go through their entire lives never having made love to a man even once," Jenny sighed.

"I hope that never happens to any of us," Laine said.

"We have a woman in our congregation everyone calls Aunt Tula, even though she's nobody's aunt," Jenny said. "She never got married. We heard she prayed that God would send her a husband but because she refused to ever wear lipstick or powder, never went anywhere but to church services, she never met anyone. Now she's ancient."

"How old is she?" Pammy asked.

"At least fifty-five."

"She always said God had a plan for her life," Laine added. "I guess that plan was to be an old maid."

"We heard Aunt Tula was told to fix herself up a little," Jenny said. "But she said if a man didn't like her the way God designed her, then she didn't want him. Her face looks like a dried up prune. And she never smiles."

"My aunt is single but my dad calls her an Unclaimed Gem," Pammy said. "Of course she's only thirty-two. I'm sure she's getting nervous though. Personally I'd rather die of a disease than never get married."

"I bet half the girls in this college have had sex," Jenny said, lowering her voice. "Here I try to hold out for the right guy and everyone I meet probably knows what it's like but me."

"Sex before marriage is a sin," Julia said. "You know that."

Pammy regarded Julia as if she had just grown a third eye.

"Well I'm Catholic but I think I'd give it up for the right guy. I mean, what if I don't meet my husband till I'm thirty? You think I'm gonna wait that long?"

"Julia, it's also a sin to think wicked thoughts but everyone does it," Jenny said, frowning. "Just thinking about sex is sinful."

"How can you think about it when you've never even done it?" Mary Lou asked.

"I can imagine it, though!" Laine said and everyone laughed. Except for Julia.

"I bet old Professor Varnerum never did it," Pammy said. "He's all hunched over and has terrible smoker's breath. He must be eighty."

"Nah, he's a widower," Mary Lou said. "And I'm sure he didn't look so bad fifty years ago. Some people do look so horrible it's a wonder anyone wants to do it with them."

"Like Professor Marblonski," Laine said. "She wears short skirts and lots of mascara and blue eye shadow. But she's a whale and her skin is awful. Pock marks everywhere! She says she's been happily married for ten years and has three kids. Who'd ever think she'd get a guy?"

"But I bet she doesn't have sex anymore," Jenny said. "I bet most people over thirty-five don't even bother. And at forty-five, nobody does."

"I think my parents still do," Pammy said. "They crack jokes and think I don't know what they mean. It's disgusting."

"Sex is for young people," Jenny said. "Don't you think, Jules? Boy, you've been quiet today. Not even giving us your opinion. By the way, did you see Professor Hunter yet?" She smirked. "Can you picture having sex with him?"

Both twins laughed.

"Who's Professor Hunter?" Mary Lou asked.

"If Julia were Catholic, I'd say she'd make a perfect nun," Pammy said. "But you Baptists don't have nuns, do you?"

"We're not Baptist," Jenny said. "We are Pentecostal. And no, we don't have nuns but we should."

"Never heard of Pent-tee-costal," Mary Lou said. "I'm half Methodist and half Catholic. My mom wouldn't care if I married a Protestant, but I wouldn't be allowed to marry an atheist."

"Pentecostal means they believe in the Holy Spirit," Laine said.

"I'm Catholic and we believe in the Trinity," Pammy said.

"Yes but we believe in tongues," Jenny said. "It's too complicated to explain. Anyway, at this point, I don't care what the guy is. He can be Buddhist as long as he's good looking."

"Now tell us what you think of Professor Hunter," Laine said, turning to Julia. "You never did let me know what you thought. He was thin, black haired and old just like I told you. Just your type!"

"But not to get married to," Jenny said. "Your type to have a date with maybe. And then you'd throw up and never like an older man again."

"What are you talking about?" Pammy said. "Who's Professor Hunter?"

"Some old teacher here who's single," Jenny said. "Julia's future husband. I think someone told me he's forty-five!"

"Yuck, too old," Mary Lou said. "You want to get married someday, right, Jules? Like us. But to a guy!"

"He's a guy," Jenny said. "Just old. Julia wants old. Don't you?"

Julia shook her head.

"At the rate you're going," Jenny said, "you'll be the last out of all of us to walk down the aisle."

"Why do you say that?" Mary Lou said. "That's kind of mean."

"I don't want to sound mean but it's true," Jenny said, jutting out her chin. "You've got to admit it, don't you, Jules, you've always gone after the wrong person. It's like you do it deliberately."

"Maybe she's just not ready for a steady guy yet," Pammy said. "You do want to get married someday, right, Julia?"

"Of course." Julia's voice sounded timid to her own ears. "I just believe certain things are just not right to do."

"But if the right person wanted you to do them, you'd change your tune," Jenny said. Her eyebrows furrowed and she looked disagreeable. "Before my mom met my dad, she said she'd never French kiss a guy. But then she told me she was so in love with our dad, he was so gorgeous, she did it."

"As if French kissing were a big thing," Laine said.

"Is that what you meant by 'tongues'?" Pammy said.

"Well back then I guess it was a big thing," Jenny said, addressing her twin. "And no, Pamela, tongues is not French kissing!"

The girls erupted in giggles.

"Maybe Julia will marry Professor Hunter one day and then she can tell us what it's all about," Mary Lou said, patting Julia's arm. "She may surprise us all."

"He's too old for her to marry," Jenny sputtered. "For heaven's sake, liking an older man is one thing, marrying one is another. Girls only marry dried up old men if they have money."

The girls nodded in agreement.

"I just know the main reason I'm even going away to college after I finish here at Raleigh is to find the right guy," Pammy said. "I don't want to spend the rest of my life working at some job. I want kids, a house, a dog, the whole deal."

"Most girls, if they're honest, don't really want careers. They want husbands and families," Laine said. "And even Donna Seerey, the smartest girl in our graduating class, said she's going to law school but she'd drop out in a second if the right guy came along."

"What's a career if you don't have love?" Pammy sighed. "Being in love with the right person has got to be the most important thing to ever happen to any girl."

"How do you know?" Mary Lou said, teasing her friend. "Are you in love and haven't told us yet?"

"I don't think Pammy's ever been in love," Jenny said. "But Julia, since we've known her, has been in love at least four times. Right Jules?"

"Yes, first there was Mr. Constantine, our geography teacher," Laine said. "Then her eye doctor -- then there was that visiting evangelist at our church, David Kristoff. He did kind of look like an older Davy Jones! And let's not forget our boss, Mr. Vratny. They were all at least fifteen years older than her."

"That isn't true," Julia said. "I wasn't in love with any of them."

"Well they were crushes," Jenny shot back.

"Look how red your face is getting," Pammy said. "Geez, Julia, you look like a beet."

"She's always turning bright red," Jenny said. "Mr. Vratny used to call her Tomato. It was his affectionate nickname for her."

"All Julia's crushes have had one thing in common," Laine said. "She called them all 'Mister'. Never by their first name. Always Mr. something or other."

"So she likes older men, that's no big deal," Mary Lou said. "I guess it's a father thing. Lots of women marry older guys. Well maybe, not lots. But some."

"Julia doesn't want a husband; she wants a father. That's what our mother says," Jenny replied. "Now let's get off the subject. I'm hungry and I have a class in ten minutes. Who wants to go to the cafeteria with me?"

* * *

"Everyone thinks you're a goody two shoes," Laine said later that afternoon when the twins were alone with Julia. "Pammy wants to know where you're ever going to meet a boyfriend the way you stay home so much. I tried to stick up for you but let's face it, Jules. Guys don't come to your door like the Avon lady. If you never go out with us, you're never going to meet someone."

"Your mother should let up on you with all the babysitting you've been doing," Jenny added. "You take care of Rob and Eddie a lot. She can't expect you to do it every Saturday night."

"I don't mind," Julia said. "I love my little brothers. It's not like my mother wants to work every Saturday night waiting tables. We need the money."

"Well, Laine and I are going out tonight with a bunch of the girls from psych class," Jenny replied. "If you change your mind and decide you want to come, give me a call. But call before six because I'll be gone by then."

"Make your plans," Julia said and turned back to her reading. "Don't let me hold you up."

Jenny flounced away, leaving Julia alone waiting for her next class.

At that moment, Julia preferred being by herself, away from the twins and their mindless chatter. The Murdens might make straight A's in all their courses but when it came to their social lives, Julia thought they were dim-witted. They tried too hard. No young man was going to go anywhere near a girl if he smelled a sense of desperation. And Laine and Jenny's quest let off a scent of despair, the stench of which frightened away even the most hapless potential suitor. Every Monday after another weekend of being without a beau, the twins would vent their sour mood on Julia.

"You're becoming nothing but a wet blanket," Jenny said one day, scowling at her best friend. "Another weekend and where were you? Pammy and I had a great time at Danfry's. I'm so glad I went there instead of Pandora's. It was disco night. Tons of guys asked to dance with us. I think one cute guy gave Pam his phone number."

"That's nice," Julia said.

"You should have been there," Jenny went on, annoyed that she failed to rattle her friend. "We all had to work Saturday but Mr. Vratny let us out early. I'm sure he let you out too but you disappeared after we punched out. And Danfry's was packed. More guys than usual showed up and they gave out free popcorn for the first hour. I think I pulled a muscle in my calf from dancing so much."

"Hmmmm," Julia said. "It sounds like you had fun."

"We sure did. I think from now on, I'm going there instead of Pandora's. I'm so sick of the same old crowd. Believe it or not, Mr. Vratny was the one who told us about it. He went there when he was young, back when they danced to swing music. Ugh."

"It was very nice of Mr. Vratny to let us all leave early," Julia said. "He's so sweet. And oh, I hope it works out with Pam and the guy she met."

"Oh, you're so happy for Pam but what about you? Don't you want to be happy for yourself for once? You stay home every night we aren't working and then when we get out of work early, you disappear. Did you go home? I hope you weren't mooning about another old guy at work," Jenny growled. "I heard they hired a new manager. And stop it with Mr. Vratny already! You know he's married. He has four kids, for heaven's sake. He looks at you as another kid. Why don't you just get over it?"

"I told you, I don't have a crush on Mr. Vratny," Julia said. "And I know he's married. Just because I think he's sweet --"

"I swear, Julia," Laine interrupted, frowning. "You definitely have a problem. Crushes were kid stuff when we were in junior high and kind of fun. We're in college now. You aren't interested in anyone. A guy comes near you and you clam up. And yet when an old man like Vratny talks to you, you look like you're in heaven. Do you want to be alone the rest of your life?"

The thought of being alone forever terrified Julia but she did not respond.

"You've got to do something about this," Jenny continued. "Our dad said you are too pretty a girl to be sitting home all the time."

"I can't help it if I'm not interested," Julia said, blinking away tears that suddenly surfaced. "The boys I meet just seem so childish."

"What do you want, some old man with grey hair? Guys are guys! They're supposed to be immature. They don't grow up till later. You don't even give anyone a chance. What is it with you? You have to be madly in love with someone before you'll even go on a date?"

"You're going to wind up having affairs with married men," Laine said. "That's what our mother said."

The twins' words stung. Julia fought back tears all the way home from class. She angrily wiped them away. No way would she let anyone know how she felt.

"Jenny and Laine again?" Mrs. Jahns remarked as Julia came into the kitchen, tossing her books on the table.

Julia shook her head.

"They depress you so much, you should think about getting other friends," her mother said. "There must be other girls in your college that you can go out with. Because lately I've noticed you're extremely down in the dumps after being with them."

"It sounds awful but right now I still need them," Julia told her.

She opened the refrigerator and got out the milk carton.

"I don't have a car and I have to get to school. Hopefully that will change once Ned fixes up an old clunker for me. At this point I don't even care how it looks on the outside as long as it runs."

Ned, her older cousin and Aunt Margie's only son, had promised her a car. He was adept at buying old cars, fixing them up and selling them. Julia had begged him to find her a cheap and reliable vehicle as soon as he had spare time.

"I've reminded Neddie you're still waiting on him," Mrs. Jahns said, wiping the kitchen table. "Maybe by next week he can sell you that old Falcon he's been working on."

"He said I can have it for two hundred dollars and that is about all I have left in my savings account."

She finished her drink, grabbed her books and went upstairs to her small attic bedroom to study. This particular night she did not have to work at Roote's. She decided to put on some music and read for class. Her five parakeets, in the cage beside her bed, began chirping at the sight of her but she was too melancholy to talk to them. Once again, tears sprung close to the surface. Tempted to watch her old home movies, she instead pulled out a textbook. She tried to concentrate, afraid if she let herself start crying she would not be able to stop.

As she opened the book, out fluttered a two part form, carbon paper separating the two pages. A smile formed on her lips. She pulled apart the two pieces of paper and stuck one in her purse. It was the receipt from the registrar's office indicating her release from speech class. Next week the new semester would begin and she was now formally enrolled in English Literature with Dr. Aiden Hunter. Even if the twins had been mistaken and Dr. Hunter was in fact a married man, Julia could still use the extra credits. But if he were single as the twins proclaimed, then she could use the adventure.

And oh, I would so love to find an older man who was by himself, she thought. Her hopes went no further than to have this professor look at her and see her as special, different from everyone else. Her bad mood lifted and she finished her homework in peace.

* * *

The beginning of the new semester fell on a balmy February day. Ned had kept his promise and presented his cousin with a 1963 Falcon just before classes started. The car's exterior had seen better days but Ned assured her that both the engine and transmission were fine.

Julia parked her new vehicle in the student lot that first day of class and looked up at the deep blue sky, so unusual for mid-winter in New Jersey. February was usually a dreary, grey and cold month. She locked the doors, pausing to catch a glimpse of her reflection in the window. A comment from Laine echoed in her mind.

"Everyone says you'd be a sharp looking girl if you'd fix yourself up a little."

Her hair, as always, hung loosely just below her chin. She never took the time to put rollers in to give it a wave. Make-up was something she did not bother with. Her blue eyes peered back at her from behind two large lenses. People often said Julia had "innocent eyes". Never knowing whether to feel complimented or insulted, she acknowledged they were correct. The twins, however, always told her it was more of an advantage to have sultry "bedroom" eyes.

Julia suddenly felt a stab of annoyance when thinking of her friends. Because they had been close for many years, Jenny and Laine Murden felt free to comment on every aspect of Julia's life. At the same time, they were thoughtful and kind, offering Julia rides to school. On her birthday and at Christmas they always presented her with generous gifts. They also had tried to find an older man for her, persuading her to enroll in Dr. Hunter's class. Julia had never heard of a love-hate friendship but it was apparent that she was in one.

On that warm winter morning in 1975, Julia did not fret long over her friends' past behavior. She walked into Professor Hunter's class and took a seat near the back of the room, feeling excited and hopeful. She watched other students arrive in class after her, the majority of them looking bored. English literature was not an interesting subject for most of them, but it was a required course for first year accounting freshmen.

A few minutes passed before Professor Hunter shuffled into the room. Posture askew, he clasped his books firmly to his side. His black eyeglasses were old and falling apart, one lens held in place by Scotch tape. He took them on and off intermittently over the next ninety minutes of class. Sometimes he would chew on them as he talked. Julia looked him over carefully. He was attractive for an older man, yet she felt a sense of uneasiness. Something was not quite right. And he looked quite a bit older than she; maybe even more than twenty years.

The twins rushed into class late that day. Breathless, they took desks on either side of Julia's. The thought of "no matter where I go, they always follow" crossed Julia's mind. But then she brushed it from her consciousness as if flicking away an annoying gnat.

"Sorry we're late," Laine said. "I told you, Jenny, I can't walk from Douglas Hall all the way over to this side of campus in just five minutes."

"You have to eat less and hurry more," Jenny replied. Douglas Hall housed the student cafeteria. "By the way, Jules, how come you ate home today? Now that you have your own car I guess we'll be seeing less of you."

Julia did not have time to answer her. Professor Hunter had cleared his throat and began writing on the board. The classroom noises quieted. Looking around, Julia noticed how few students were in the room. No one liked an eight a.m. class and few had signed up.

"My name is Dr. Aiden Hunter," Professor Hunter said, looking down at his books as he stood before his desk. "Forgive me if I don't pronounce all your names correctly or if I ever get around to memorizing them at all. I will now call roll to make sure you are where you are supposed to be."

He sat down at the desk and pulled out a black binder. His voice a monotone, he began to read the names listed, rolling out the words as if he were bored:

"Misssssssssssssssssssss Adamsssssssssssssss, Mr. Boccinoooooooooooooo, Mr. Deckerrrrrrrrrrrrrrrrrrrrrrrrr, Mr. Elliottttttttttttttttttttt".

"Now," he continued after roll was called, "if I appear half-hearted today it is due to the fact I've just recovered from an illness which necessitated my hospitalization last month during winter break. My doctor has allowed me to come back to class but I am not yet my old self. Not that the old self was much more charismatic," and he smiled a small smile, waving his hand in the air.

"Oh my gosh, Julia, look how little his feet are!" Jenny said in a loud whisper.

A few students sitting nearby gave her a quizzical look. Julia followed her gaze. The professor's off white, black laced shoes were visible from beneath the desk.

"So what?" Julia thought, but she said nothing.

Professor Hunter appeared too small for his rumpled denim leisure suit. He looked to Julia to be a man who neither cared how he looked or what he wore. His face was pasty white, in sharp contrast with ebony black hair. Dark eyes that were big and solemn looked sadly out at the world, encircled in purple shadows. Never had Julia seen anyone look more ethereal. Why, he looked like a poet and she found that both pitiable and appealing. She leaned further in her seat, her hand on her chin, studying him.

"She'll be in love in no time," Laine whispered to her sister. "Look at her! He's her type all right."

"And no wedding band on his finger," Jenny said, grinning.

"Shhhh," Julia admonished.

"Next time I'm sitting up in the front row," Jenny said. "I can't see the board and I refuse to wear my glasses."

"Vanity, vanity," Laine said, rolling her eyes. "Okay, let's all sit up front next time."

The twins both nodded, assuming Julia was in agreement. They began passing notes to one another, oblivious to Aiden Hunter and his lesson. Opening his literature book, Professor Hunter began to read. Several students yawned and took notes. Though not English born, Aiden Hunter spoke in a clipped British voice. He then would pause and look up at the class, as if not trusting them to pay attention. He commented on what he was reading, then asked what the class thought. He did not seem to think it odd that no one responded. Several times he made remarks under his breath. He muttered to himself, then smiled, as if he were accustomed to being alone and content with his own company.

"Now," he said, closing the book. "I would like each of you to write me a paragraph or two as to why you feel the study of English literature is still relevant for today. And tell me a bit about yourselves. Keep it brief. And keep it honest. I will see you Thursday."

Julia glanced at the clock, surprised the class was over. Professor Hunter had grabbed his books and left the room. Jenny got up slowly, adjusting her pocketbook strap on her shoulder.

"Glad that's over with," she said. "I'm going back to Douglas Hall to see if Craig showed up."

Craig McCrory was a young man Jenny had discovered the previous semester in one of her classes. Smitten by his good looks, she hoped he would soon ask her out.

"You guys coming with me?"

Laine nodded, grabbing Julia's arm.

"Sure," she said. "By the way, I heard some bad news. Roote's might be going out of business."

Julia, who had been daydreaming about Professor Hunter, suddenly realized what her friend had said.

"What?" she said, eyes widening. "Please tell me that's just a rumor! I need that job!"

"I stopped by the store last night to pick up my check and heard Dolores talking to Mr. Vratny. Roote's might close next month, or even sooner. But don't worry, we can all get other part-time jobs pretty fast. Stores are always looking to hire college kids. We can have our pick."

"But I liked Roote's," Jenny whined.

Julia agreed. Roote's was a fun place to work. Most of the other employees were young adults. Dolores, the fifty-five year old supervisor, was cantankerous at times but she enjoyed playing mother hen to all her "kids". Mr. Vratny, thirty-eight years old, was Dolores' boss. Julia enjoyed working when he was there. He was kind-hearted, always smiled and paid attention to her in a fatherly way.

"If you hear anything more, let me know," Julia told Jenny. "I just have to have another job right away."

"You're going to miss Mr. Vratny more than the job," Laine smirked. "But it was a fun job and I'm going to miss it too. And we got to work together. Let's try to find another job where we can still be together."

The following morning, the twins telephoned Julia to tell her Roote's was indeed closing.

"But not for two months," Jenny said. "So we've got time."

Laine, who was listening on the extension, added, "I hear Raleigh is offering a work-study program to students like us who need financial aid. It would mean working for a professor, doing stuff like Xeroxing or typing. Why don't we all apply? We can work on-campus. Sure will save us money not having use our cars to go back and forth."

"I'm not interested," Jenny said. "I'm in school too much as it is. But maybe Julia would love that. Maybe she can work with Professor Hunter."

Both twins laughed.

"By the way, Jules, you never really told us what you thought of him," Laine said. "Old man Hunter, your future fiancé! Wasn't I right? He's just your type."

"One foot in the grave and the other on a banana peel," Jenny chirped.

"He's cute," Julia admitted, ignoring the teasing. "And he does have a baby face. But just because he doesn't wear a wedding band doesn't mean he's not married."

"I already told you, dummy, he's definitely not married," Jenny replied. "When I was at that student forum last fall, he was introduced as one of the faculty. The president made a joke about him being a bachelor. Good grief, don't you ever listen? By the way Julia, getting off the old man subject, Craig's friend Louis bumped into me this morning in the parking lot. Remember I told you about him?"

"No."

"Yes you do. He's older than us. Craig said he's around twenty-six. He met him in one day in the cafeteria and they've been hanging out. Craig thinks he's a real nice guy.

"Uh-huh."

"You must remember him, Jules, he's got platinum blond hair. Why he's almost an albino! But on him, it looks really cute. And he's got these gorgeous aquamarine colored eyes. Anyway, Craig is now friends with him. He's even gotten him into some bars."

"That's nice."

"Anyway, it's weird," Jenny continued. "Being as you're so quiet and let's face it, we're not widely known around here. But Louis knew you. Craig saw both of us one day and pointed me out. But Louis said he knew YOU. He said he saw you when you were switching from your speech class to take Hunter's lit class. He had overheard the registrar asking you why you were taking English Literature when you didn't need it to fulfill your major. I guess he was behind you in line."

"Knows me? I don't think so," Julia said.

"You know what I mean. He recognized you. Maybe he likes you. Listen, he's a cute guy and he's older. He's twenty-six. This might be a good thing."

"Hmmm," Julia said, her mind going back to Professor Hunter.

"Anyway Craig told him you liked old men," Jenny continued. "Sorry Jules, but I told Craig that you did. I think Craig even told him you took Hunter's class because he was single."

"Now why would you do that?" Julia said, suddenly annoyed.

"Well, it is true. That's why you took the class. Anyway, forget about that. I'm glad Craig told Louis you liked old men. Maybe he'll ask you out. Craig said he doesn't date much, he likes straight girls, and no one is straighter than you. Wouldn't it be great, I'll date Craig and we can double-date, you with Louis! I'm working on Craig. Every day now we're talking or going to the cafeteria."

"I don't know," Julia said. "I'm sure Louis is a nice guy but why is he still going to a junior college when he's twenty-six?"

"How would I know?"

Jenny went on to list all her grievances about why Craig had not yet asked her out. Julia said "I know" and "uh-huh" at the appropriate times but her mind wandered.

Work on campus? Julia thought. Why, of course. Not only would she save on auto expenses but she would be able to get closer to Professor Hunter. Maybe even work for him! And get paid to do so. What could be more perfect?

Finally certain he was unwed, she began daydreaming. Her head was full of romantic fancying. She pictured his face close to hers, his dark eyes peering into her own.

"Hey, are you two listening?" Laine said. "I want us to figure out what we're going to do for money, which we all need desperately. Forget Craig and Louis right now. Let's apply for the campus jobs. They're setting up a desk now in the student lounge to take applications. I want us to apply today. I don't want to forget about this and then we're stuck with no job at all."

"Count me out," Jenny said.

"I'll do it," Julia said.

Laine pushed her twin to reconsider. Break up the threesome? It seemed horrifying. Jenny relented, with reluctance.

* * *

Laine, Jenny and Julia stood in front of a make-shift desk in the corner of the student lounge. The registrar handing out applications for student jobs looked at the three young women in front of her and cackled.

A well-preserved sixty, Sandee had been working for Raleigh College for many years. She had once been an ordinary housewife raising three offspring, but after her husband left when her kids were teenagers, she was forced to get a job. In the 1950s, forty-plus women didn't have a lot of choices. Sandee went from driving a school bus to licking stamps at a mailing facility. It was sheer luck that someone was able to get her at job at the college. Sandee's mantra in life was no longer God, Family, Country but rather Family (and that was limited to a select few), the Democratic Party and in third place, God. These days, she found herself growing more disenchanted with her Catholic faith. She began to pigeon-hole the Almighty into nothing but a male chauvinist, if only in spirit form. Sandee felt she had gotten a raw deal in life and blamed her heavenly Father for a lot of it.

Though disgruntled with her life story, Sandee was grateful for her looks. Frosted, shoulder-length tawny hair, high cheekbones and almond shaped hazel eyes made her appear younger than her years. Her deep smoker's voice, a voice she deemed sexy, resonated when she spoke, causing people passing by to glance over at her. A polyester leopard print blouse hugged her ample bosom and emphasized a twenty-eight inch waist. Around her neck was an orange scarf, hiding what she called her chicken neck. Though her ensemble appeared brighter than most of the other female support staff, mostly made up of matronly women, Sandee enjoyed her sense of style. She had once been a very attractive woman who planned on hanging on to those good looks for as long as possible.

"Well, luvs, it seems we have a sudden interest in the work-study," she said, smiling so that the laugh lines around her eyes deepened. "It's rather boring work, so I've heard, as these professors can be, ahem, somewhat stodgy, but it is a paying job. We don't have many young ones wanting to work here so I'm glad to meet you three. And you look eager enough. By the way, I'm Mrs. Dee – you can call me Sandee – and you'll be getting paychecks every week from moi if you decide to take the job."

"Sandee Dee?" said Laine. "Is that your real name?"

"Afraid so, luv," Sandee said, rifling through papers and handing each girl a form. "My maiden name was Blasio. I married a fella named Dominick Dee, 'way back in 1934. His parents were from Calabria and Dee was some guinea name he shortened. A liar from day one!"

She laughed so loud others in the lounge stopped and stared.

"I'm Italian myself so I can say that!"

"Oh, okay," Jenny said, thrown off by such a lack of pretense. "Nice to meet you. And yes, we'd really like to work here. But we want to stay together, the three of us, if we can. We all worked for the same store part-time but it's closing soon."

"What are you, the Boppsy triplets? Or were the three of you once all conjoined at birth?"

"No, I mean, yes. I mean, the two of us are twin sisters and Julia is our best friend." Jenny did not realize Sandee was joking. "Can you please let us know today if we definitely will get these jobs?"

"I can let you know soon. These jobs would start in about two weeks. Just stop back by my desk to find out if you've been accepted but I'm sure there'll be no problem. I know we have one work-study opening in the English department. That one would require someone on Mondays and Fridays. Aiden Hunter needs help badly, he is so disorganized and if you ask me, they should hire an exterminator too just to clean out his office."

"Oh, we'll let Julia have that assignment," Jenny said, elbowing her sister. "She'd be the perfect candidate."

"And we'll take whatever else you have," Laine added.

Sandee looked over at Julia who was blushing and clutching books tightly against her chest.

"So you are Julia I am surmising? And you have a mad desire to work in the English department? Have you ever even encountered Dr. Hunter? Seen his office? Because after that experience, I doubt any young lady of your attractiveness would want to go anywhere near him!"

Laine and Jenny erupted in giggles. Julia felt her face turn redder.

"She thinks there's a chance she might fall in love with Dr. Hunter," Laine said. "But don't tell him. I mean, she doesn't want him to know just yet."

Jenny laughed louder, unaware of her friend's embarrassment.

Sandee gave Julia a sympathetic yet stunned look.

"Fall in love? Dr. Hunter? Are we talking about the same man? Why he's deep into his forties and you girls look no more than teenagers. Now don't think I'm a rumormonger, but he's an odd one. Keeps to himself, even at school, and lives alone. No girlfriend, not even a dog. Some say he drinks quite a bit. Of course, I know they're just rumors. But where's there's smoke, there's usually fire. He's not exactly my cup of tea but then, I've never had a man shortage my entire life and at your age, I used to have to beat them away with a stick!"

She broke into loud laughter once again. Jenny and Laine smiled in amusement but Julia was mortified. What if she screamed Dr. Hunter's name when he was nearby?

"To each his own, though," Sandee added, grinning at Julia. "Don't let any friends dissuade you if you think you're in love. But Dr. Hunter? You must have the wrong man. He's far too old for the likes of you. Chase the young fellas. And follow your heart, I always say. I should've done that and I would have been better off. I married a real El Creepo and the bum ran around on me the whole twenty-plus years I was married to him. Make sure you know what you're getting into, girls, before you get that ring on your finger. Follow your heart, yes, but follow him around the first few weeks. Sure will save you a lot of heartache."

"So your husband was a cheat?" Jenny said.

"He got his wandering ways from his best friend, Vernon," Sandee replied. "I called him Vermin! He was nothing but a no-good hillbilly from Georgia. Mix a Good Ole Boy with a guinea and you have a recipe for disaster!"

"Our mothers are divorced," Jenny said. "We know a little of what bad marriages are like."

"Oh is that so," Sandee said. "My own kids haven't seen their father in many years. He ran off with someone from the roller derby – fancied herself another Montana Jean Payne. Ugly girl with red hair and freckles. Big woman, wore a size sixteen. Heard they're living in Florida. Well, she can have him. I'm through with him and all men. But after my divorce, I had so many boyfriends I thought I'd die of exhaustion. Now, at my present age – I'm sixty, would you believe it – I still get winked at. I've kept the figure I had at twenty-five. My son's friend even made a pass at me, thought I was Vinnie's sister. Ha, if you got it, I guess you never lose it."

As the girls filled out the applications, Sandee was lost in thought, remembering her glory days.

"Well, that was another era. I probably should have remarried then I wouldn't still have to be working. Not that this place is so bad."

The girls finished the forms and handed them to Sandee.

"It was sure nice chatting with you," Sandee said, even though she had done most of the talking. "I'll put your requests through and expedite them. You girls have been wonderful, listening to me go on, nicer than my own kids."

She turned to wink at Julia.

"And luv, I'll be sure to arrange it so you can work for Professor Hunter. Though Lord knows why anyone would want that!"

"Thank you so much," Laine said.

"Yes, thank you," Julia whispered, lowering her eyes.

Later that day, Julia went over the conversation with Sandee. She had been embarrassed yet exhilarated to hear her name intertwined with Dr. Hunter's. Picturing herself wrapped in his embrace, Julia went through the rest of her day barely hearing what anyone said to her. Maybe that crazy Sandee lady would tell her professor what the twins had said. Maybe it was a good thing after all that the twins liked to gossip. Thanks to them, she now knew that Professor Hunter was not only a man alone, but he did not even have a girlfriend. It was too good to be true. After years of looking for an older man to call her own, Julia felt she had hit the mother lode. She ignored Sandee's comments about the alcohol. Many people drank, it was no big deal. Maybe Dr. Hunter drank out of loneliness. Whatever was said, Julia concentrated on one fact: Dr. Aiden Hunter was an older man who had no wife, no kids, no anyone.

The girls went to work that evening optimistic that they would soon have new jobs. Their coworkers, disheartened, all gathered around the main register talking with Dolores and Mr. Vratny. Roote's would soon be no more. It had been a fixture in the town of Crane Ridge since Julia's grandparents were young.

Julia stood off to the side, her head in the clouds as she pictured herself working with Dr. Hunter. She did not notice Mr. Vratny walk over to her. He put an arm around her shoulder.

"Don't worry," he said. "I'm sure you girls will all find new jobs. I'll make sure you all get a great recommendation."

Jenny and Laine snickered. While Julia warmed to her boss's attention, she was irritated once again at her friends' behavior.

"I'm not worried," she said to Mr. Vratny, smiling. "These things sometimes happen."

"All things happen for a reason," Dolores said, her voice soothing. "God will always open another door after one closes."

* * *

As the days wore on, Julia closely observed Professor Hunter in class, taking note of every word, every mannerism. No one else around her paid the least bit attention to his lectures which often went off in tangential circles. He was star-struck and spoke of his love of attending the theatre, movies and plays. His eyes would sparkle when he mentioned spotting a famous person on the streets of New York City, not far from the New Jersey town in which he lived.

"I just adore popcorn," he said one day. "I am also quite addicted to chocolate."

"That's not all he looks like he's addicted to," a boy sitting behind Julia whispered. "Whew, don't light a match around this guy."

Julia ignored the comment. As soon as she was able, she went to the store and bought several bags of popcorn and chocolate kisses. Each morning before Professor Hunter arrived at school, Julia put some popcorn in a paper cup and left it on his desk beside his mug. In class, he never mentioned the popcorn. Then Julia started leaving him a solitary chocolate candy kiss. For several days he did not mention that either.

Julia and the twins were now sitting in the front row, directly in front of Aiden Hunter, who liked to read from his book sitting atop the desk, swinging his legs. Julia would spend the ninety minutes of class studying his face, analyzing his every word, while the twins giggled and wrote notes.

Why do you do that, Julia thought one day, embarrassed the girls sat near her. *It's so rude to ignore this man who is trying to teach a class.*

One morning Professor Hunter abruptly stopped reading aloud and slammed the book shut. The sound made the sleepy class jump. Laine and Jenny stopped their whispered conversation to look at him, startled. Julia, who had never stopped watching him, smiled.

For sure he's going to yell at those twins, she thought, hopeful.

But he did not.

Professor Hunter put the book down on his desk and rose to his feet. His dark eyes blackened behind his glasses and he pursed his lips. It was as if he were trying to decide whether to say what he was thinking or keep it to himself.

"She left a kiss within my cup!" he exclaimed and because he was usually soft-spoken, everyone now paid him full attention.

"What?" Jenny turned to her sister, her eyes widening.

Professor Hunter gazed at Julia.

"She left a kiss within my cup" he repeated, his voice softening.

Julia, aware the twins did not know she left chocolate kisses on his desk, bowed her head. Her face felt hot. Jenny nudged her and said "What's the matter with you?"

Julia raised her eyes and met her professor's eyes. They regarded each other for several seconds and then he looked away.

As if it had never happened, he picked up his book, sat back down on the desk and proceeded reading aloud. The classroom settled back down to its inattentiveness and Jenny and Laine returned to their note-writing. Only Julia felt exhilarated. The colors in the room seemed to be more vibrant, the sun shining in through the window felt warmer and brilliantly gold.

He knew it was her. He knew! The glow of their mutual secret stayed with her the rest of the day.

CHAPTER THREE

He was almost five years old, walking with his mother and younger brother through a big meadow. Mother had his hand in hers while her younger son, Guenther, leaped and ran ahead. When they came to a spot she liked, Mother put down a blanket and picnic basket. Guenther was busy chasing an imaginary playmate but the little boy stayed by his mother's side, stroking her hand.

"Let me loose now," Mother coaxed, "And go pick flowers with your brother."

Hesitating at first, the little boy obeyed. He was glad Mama was smiling today. Sometimes he'd find her crying and he'd climb into her lap and hold her face in his hands. "What's wrong?" he would ask. "I miss baby George today," she'd tell him.

For a long time, he did not know who baby George was. He thought he, not George, was the oldest son. But today was a good day. Mama was happy and they were having lunch together in the field. The two boys picked dandelions and presented their mother with a large bouquet. She clapped her hands in delight. "How very beautiful they are!" she cried. "We'll have such a pretty supper table tonight, won't we?"

The boy's heart swelled at his mother's pleasure. When he was a grown-up man, he thought, he was going to marry her and always give her flowers.

One cloudy, mild February morning, Julia began her day by oversleeping. *Of all times to be tired*, she scolded herself. *Idiot! Idiot!* She checked her alarm clock, which had indeed gone off, then rushed through her morning routine, glad no one was in the bathroom to slow her down.

Today was a special day. Today was going to be exciting even though the weather was gloomy and it was February, a most hated month. Because today was her student-teacher conference with Professor Hunter. He had asked his students to each schedule a time to meet with him privately and as far as she knew, she was the only one who had. The twins were not interested. It had been a request, not an order. If their grade would not be affected, they did not want to go.

"You're probably the only student who is seeing him," Laine had said. "He's going to know you like him just on that alone."

"Wedding bells are not far off," Jenny had added.

The twins were in a good mood. Sandee had phoned them and said all three girls were now accepted in the work-study program. Jenny had smirked when she discovered Julia would be working with Professor Hunter.

"Ugh, ugh, he's ugh-lee," Jenny said. "But I guess you're thrilled now, Jules. You'll be close enough to him to count every wrinkle."

"Seriously," Laine said. "What if he asks you out? I mean, really, it could happen. Older men are flattered by young girls. Our mother said this might backfire on you and he falls in love. Then what would you do? Because you wouldn't ever really want to get involved with someone like that. But then our mother also asked why he's still single. Maybe he's got a wife he left or even one he never divorced."

"Nah, he's an old maid in pants," Jenny said. "He's never been married. As far as anybody knows, he is alone. And after being in his class these few weeks, I can see why. What a bore!"

Julia did not see Aiden Hunter as a bore. Jenny's words floated into the air and around her head. But Laine's words delighted her. *What if he fell in love,* she thought. *With me!* She smiled and the twins thought she was enjoying their disparaging remarks.

Now, as she drove the short distance to the school, black storm clouds overhead caught her attention. "How strange to have such warm weather in February," she thought. Thunder boomed, followed by a brilliant flash of lightning. Fat raindrops began splashing across the windshield. She was four blocks from the college when the downpour began. Julia reduced her speed then slowed to a crawl when something caught her eye.

A small male figure walked along the side of the road, quickening his steps as the rain increased. He carried no overcoat or umbrella and his head was bowed. Julia strained her eyes to see who it was when to her surprise, she realized it was Professor Hunter. She pulled her car over to the side of the road, rolled down the window and yelled out to him.

"Excuse me! Would you like a ride?"

Aiden Hunter's rapid trot came to a stop and he looked around to see who had spoken. Shielding his head with a rolled up newspaper, he turned to see a young woman in an old car.

"I'm on my way to Raleigh," Julia called out. "I'm one of your students. I can give you a ride so you don't get drenched."

Julia could not believe the words that came out of her mouth. It was if she were watching herself act out a part in a movie. Too shy to even speak out in class, she was now asking her professor to climb inside her vehicle!

Aiden paused. Then, as if written into a script, there was another loud clap of thunder. The sky lit up. That was all he needed. He ran over to the car and opened the passenger door.

"Well," he said, out of breath from the sudden exertion. "Was that good timing or was that good timing?"

He arranged his newspaper at his feet and looked over at his benefactor. Squinting his eyes, he recognized his student. A smile formed on his lips.

"Hmmmmm, I believe you are Miss – Miss --"

"Jahns," Julia said.

"Ah, yes, Jahns. My early class. The class with those tittering identical females."

"You mean my friends, Elaine and Jennifer Murden."

"Yes, well, whatever their names are. They seem to find my class amusing and rarely pull out a pen to take a note."

How true, Julia thought. She was glad he looked annoyed. She wanted him to dislike the twins.

As she pulled back out into traffic, thunder boomed and the skies opened up. Aiden Hunter rolled up the window which had been slightly open but Julia did not even notice the rain.

"I appreciate your picking me up," Aiden said. "My, my, maybe we should invest in an ark. It's just awful out there. My car is in the shop once again so I had to take mass transit and walk from the train station."

Julia felt shy. She was glad her eyes were on the road so she did not have to look at him.

"I was just accepted into the work-study program," she said after a pause. "I guess you know about it? They assigned me to the English department which means I'll be assisting you and Mrs. Calgenero."

"Is that so? No one mentioned it to me."

"Mrs. Dee told us about it. Anyway, it's only going to be for a few hours on Mondays and Fridays. I'm basically a paid gopher, helping with mimeographing and typing. I think it starts next week."

"All for the minimum wage? Hmmmmm, well I suppose any income does help the proverbial struggling student. I myself worked part-time when I was in college."

Julia nodded, then remembered his classroom outburst regarding the chocolate kiss. She hoped he would not mention it. She need not have worried. As they approached the Raleigh parking lot, Aiden Hunter bent down to retrieve his newspaper.

"You can let me off right here," he said, pointing to the side wing of the building. "I thank you so very much."

Julia pulled over and watched him get out.

"That's okay," she said and a clap of thunder exploded as she spoke.

Aiden Hunter turned to give her a last look.

"It seems we're written in the stars," he said, and left her to ponder his meaning.

* * *

At four o'clock that afternoon, Julia knocked on Aiden Hunter's office door. He was puffing on a cigarette and sipping tea, engrossed in his reading.

"What are you doing here?" he said, looking at her over the rim of his cup. "Isn't it Tuesday?"

The abrupt reaction surprised and frightened Julia, and he immediately felt an emotion he rarely entertained: empathy.

"I'm sorry," he said gently. "Come in, please."

"I, I have an appointment with you."

How quickly he could make her feel ill at ease. She realized he had forgotten the scheduled student-teacher conferences that week.

"The conference," Julia said. "I'm supposed to ---"

"Oh yes, sorry," Aiden said. "Please come in and sit down."

Julia closed the office door and took a seat on the armchair opposite his desk.

"My apologies," Aiden said, glancing down at his date book. "Miss Jahns, four o'clock. Your student conference. My mistake."

Julia watched him as he shuffled papers around, grabbing a folder with her name on it. His hair was tousled and his face pale, a blotch of red coloring the tip of his nose. Julia had heard her fellow classmates snickering about his nose, saying the discoloration was a sure sign he was a drunk. In class she had never noticed his fragility. Now, sitting this near to him, with the sun streaming in from the large window at his back, sudden pity swept over her.

"Miss Jahns, Miss Jahns," he murmured, rifling through a pile of her work. "Like most of my students, you don't know how to spell. However, your writing is quite good. Sophisticated. Do you enjoy writing?"

"Yes," Julia said. "I wrote more when I was younger, but now ---"

"*Younger?*" he interrupted, raising an eyebrow. "Why, you're what --- only twenty?"

"Almost nineteen. I don't write as much as I used to. In junior high, I wrote all the time, sometimes I'd stay up till two in the morning typing stories on my typewriter."

"Hmmmmmmmm."

There was a prolonged silence.

"I guess I didn't write because I thought I was very good at it. I did it because I find it's a good way to --- to help yourself emotionally. Good therapy for your soul."

"And you felt you needed some sort of therapy?"

"Y-y-yes. I guess. You see, my parents got a divorce when I was in junior high and I wrote a lot of stories about that."

"About what?"

"About children left wounded by divorce."

"And you were wounded?"

Julia felt uncomfortable. The conversation was getting too close to her pain. She lowered her eyes.

"Sometimes."

Aiden, who rarely noticed anyone else's feelings beyond his own, realized he had been too intrusive. To his surprise, her melancholy softened him. No longer wanting to pry further, he changed the subject.

"Yes, well, your writing shows potential. You might want to look into that field as a profession. I understand you are aiming to become a kindergarten teacher?"

"That's what my guidance counselor told me I should be. Back in high school. I don't know if I really want to do that. I mean, I don't know even if I like children all that much."

"I detest children," he said, frowning. "Most of them are nothing more than little monsters."

"Well, I don't know about that. I mean, we were all children once. I just don't know if I like them enough to want to cope with them all day long."

"Yes, well, I suppose you want to marry someday and produce a passel of them yourself," he said. "In that case, you would be better off majoring in journalism. You could freelance. Now, I've read both your essay on why you feel English literature is still relevant today and this synopsis about yourself. You believe the study of literature is as important to today's writing in the same way the study of history is to present-day current events. Hmmmm, interesting. And in your autobiography paragraph, you write that you are not very social or athletic, you prefer to read books over attending parties, and you own five parrots."

"Parakeets. Yes, I've had them for years. I love my birds. All birds, in fact. They're not only beautiful on the outside but their eyes look as if they hold wisdom. It's as if they know thing people cannot know. But I guess that sounds silly."

"Not at all."

Aiden observed his reticent student become animated. Something stirred in him when he looked at her. What was it?

"I must comment," he said, "that for a college student not to desire incessant partying is a rarity indeed. And admirable. Anyway, getting back to other matters, I believe your writing shows some talent and I feel that I must advise you to develop ---"

He stopped in mid-sentence, suddenly confused.

"Before I proceed, I must tell you. I've neglected to properly thank you for that ride to school. No doubt you saved me from likely electrocution. My car seems to be in the throes of demise and I find myself at the mercy of nature these days."

Taken aback by the abrupt chance of topic, Julia said, "You don't have to thank me. I saw you walking and the rain started and I knew, well, of course, since I knew you, I, I …"

She was nervous, unable to continue. His eyes watched her with eagerness.

"And you what?" he said

"I --- I ---"

She could not finish her thought. His gaze made her panic.

"I'd like to treat you to a cup of coffee, or perhaps tea if that's your preference, for the good deed you bestowed on me today," he said. The words popped out of his mouth, surprising him. What was he doing? He never took anyone out for coffee. He hated coffee and he hated small talk.

Julia blushed, annoyed with herself for her lack of composure.

"You are turning quite red, Miss Jahns. No need to feel you have to take me up on my offer."

"No, I always turn red, it's --- well, of course, I could go out for a cup of coffee."

She looked down at her hands, strands of hair covering her eyes.

"I know you could go. What I am proposing is perhaps you would go. What is a good time for you to take your lunch break? Tomorrow, that is."

"Around one I guess."

"I've seen you in the cafeteria at noon most days. Those friends of yours going to object?"

Julia knew he disliked Jenny and Laine. On days they were not in class, he would wave his hand at their empty desks and say "those two misanthropes not showing today?"

"No, they have nothing to say about what I do."

"All right then, come by my office tomorrow at one o'clock. We can visit the coffee shop down the street. If that's to your liking."

"Fine," she said, arising. She found it hard to catch her breath. The atmosphere in the room had changed. She wanted to leave.

"I have to go now. But thank you --- thanks for telling me I have a chance for a writing career."

He stood up and nodded.

There was silence as he watched her gather her books. Then he smiled. For some reason he felt wistful. His eyes flickered with a distant memory, too far back to be clear in his own mind. And Julia was too flustered to notice anything but her own embarrassment.

* * *

Julia had a hard time getting through the rest of the day. She could not believe she was going out with her professor. Almost like a date! Well, not almost but it was the most surreal thing she had ever experienced. First he was telling her she could be a writer and the next thing she knew, he had asked her out. Because going to a coffee shop outside of campus was not what a professor would normally ask of a student. Was it? She tried hard to recall if any other student had gone for coffee with a teacher. So engrossed in thought, Julia had bumped into a wall while walking to her next class. She felt as if she were floating, like a sleepwalker in the midst of a heavenly dream, and did not answer the twins when they peppered her with questions. Instead, she changed the subject, asking about their plans for that weekend. It didn't take much to divert Jenny or Laine's line of thought.

True to his word, Aiden Hunter was standing by his office door at one o'clock the following day. He pulled on his watchband as she made her way over to him, her stomach in knots. She felt pale as if the blood had drained from her face. If she had been any other person, she would have noticed Aiden Hunter's rumpled appearance. His orange shirt was wrinkled under an ill-fitting polyester suit jacket. Dingy white shoes peeked out beneath trousers in need of a hemming. His eyes had a distracted look. Julia saw none of this. His age, to her, was his most attractive feature.

"It's too nice to take the car," he said without a greeting. "Why don't we walk?"

"Okay," Julia said. "If we're going to Ye Coffee Shoppe, it's only four blocks away."

"Short blocks," Aiden said.

They left campus together, walking toward the main avenue that led to the center of town. Crane Ridge had several streets made up of various small stores and shops. Julia normally visited downtown on weekends when it was bustling with people. Today, however, all was quiet.

Both said little during their walk and Julia was surprised at her professor's pace. She had difficulty keeping up with him. They arrived at the coffee shop and he held the door for her. He led her to a booth by a window and motioned for a waitress. Julia looked around, curious to see if there were anyone she knew. Aiden picked up a menu and frowned.

"I don't usually go out for coffee --- or lunch --- at all," he said. "I prefer to eat at my desk. But I've stopped here for a sandwich a few times. Their food isn't bad."

"And how is their coffee?"

"Since I drink tea, I have no idea. But I've heard favorable things."

Putting the menu down, he noticed the waitress filling both their cups with coffee without asking them what they wanted. She dashed away before Aiden could inform her that he wanted tea. He rolled his eyes and Julia smiled.

"Well, Miss Jahns," he said, after the waitress had retreated. "I am glad you were able to accompany me today. And I would like to ask you a question, hopefully not appearing as intrusive as I was at our last meeting. I was just curious as to why you're taking my class."

"Your class?"

His question startled her. Taken aback, she soon realized that like her, he too appeared nervous and shy. He clasped his hands together so that the knuckles whitened. His eyes were lowered as he spoke. The sunny glow from the window cast a beam of light on their table and as Julia toyed with her school ring, it sparkled.

"Yes. I see from your records, and what you tell me, you're majoring in education. You need speech class to fulfil that major, hmmmmm?"

"Why, yes. I guess I do. I just --- well, when I . . ."

Her voice trailed off.

"Never mind, you don't have to give me a reason. I suppose you just have a great love for the English poets."

She did not know if he were joking but she felt her face burn. Sudden anxiety made the coffee in front of her look unappealing. *If I take a sip, I might throw up.*

"Those friends of yours," Aiden said, opening a sugar packet and emptying it into his cup. "Why are you so intimidated by them?"

"Jenny and Laine?" She was glad he changed the subject. "Why, I'm not."

"Don't let them bully you. There are times you are hesitant to speak."

"In class? Well, sometimes I feel I'll say the wrong thing."

"And so what if you do?"

"Then I'll be embarrassed."

"At what? What do you care what other people think? Why indeed? People are always going to think something, you can't prevent it. You might as well be honest and say what you think."

"I, I --- I know. Sometimes it's hard for me."

"A lot of that difficulty will change with maturity. Not that I'm implying you're immature."

He raised the coffee cup to his nose and made a face.

"Smells bitter. I am remembering why I never order coffee," he said. A silence ensued until the waitress returned to ask if they would like anything else.

"A BLT for me," Aiden said, "on white bread, please. And Miss Jahns?"

"Just a corn muffin," Julia replied. Her stomach starting to ache, she forced herself to take a sip of her coffee.

"You aren't like all the others," he said after the waitress had left. "I've noticed a sophistication among the young people here on the east coast. You have that too. Yet you are different, less worldly."

"Well, I don't smoke or drink," Julia said. "My friends think I'm very old fashioned. They don't like that about me."

"I see. And what they think bothers you?"

She shrugged.

"I guess it does some of the time. So you think the east coast students are different?"

"I'm from the midwest --- Nebraska. Life there is simpler, much slower moving. People are more 'salt of the earth' and wary of strangers. On the contrary, being a stranger here in New Jersey is the normal way of life. But it's been a long time since I was back in Nebraska."

"Do you have family there?"

"My father died ten years ago. I have a younger brother who lives in Lincoln. He calls but doesn't come east too often. He's a pediatrician."

"What about your mother?"

"She died when I was five years old. I also had a brother who died as a small child. My parents, so I heard, never got over it."

"That's so sad," Julia said, losing her nervousness as she thought about his loss. "I have two younger brothers. I'd be crushed if something happened to either one of them."

"I never knew this brother. He passed away from pneumonia when I was six months old. He was only two."

The waitress reappeared and left a bill in front of Aiden's plate along with his sandwich.

"And where's your corn muffin?" Aiden said.

"Never mind," Julia replied. "It's okay. Don't call her back over."

"You are sure?"

Julia nodded, forcing the coffee cup to her lips.

"My recuperation has been slow," Aiden said, taking a bite out of his sandwich and then pushing it aside. "My appetite has not yet fully returned."

"Yes, you said you were sick over winter break," Julia said. "I hope it wasn't serious."

"A viral infection of some sort," Aiden shrugged. "Doctors don't know where or how I picked it up. Who knows? I've never trusted doctors. I spent two weeks in the hospital and I might as well have been at home. The one time my doctor stuck his head in the door, I was in the shower. But that is neither here nor there. I made sure I rested and felt fortunate that I did not have to miss work."

Julia nodded, taking note that his brother was a doctor and yet he did not trust doctors.

Aiden took another two bites of his sandwich, wiped his mouth with a napkin, then abruptly stood up.

"Ready?"

Julia nodded. She followed him to the cash register where he paid their bill.

The walk back to school was too short for Julia. She was no longer nervous, the tight knot in her stomach loosening. Aiden Hunter fascinated her. He was older, mysterious and carried a sad aura. Yet she could sense he liked her and enjoyed talking to her.

"I'm not really crazy about those twins," Julia said as they walked (and this time she noticed Aiden had slowed his frantic pace). "I really hate the way they act in your class. They're so silly. And they criticize me a lot."

"If they are so tormenting, why do you remain their friend?"

"I'm not sure. I've known them since I was thirteen."

"Ah, so you share a past history."

"Yes and well, our mothers know each other and are friendly, they go to the same church as we do, and it's just that ---"

She stopped in confusion. Why *did* she continue the relationship with them?

"So they are a habit."

"I guess so."

He was quiet. This time the silence between them did not feel the least bit awkward.

"Habits die hard," Aiden said. "They're almost like superstitions. You know, I had a superstitious grandmother. Not only did she attend every funeral in the county, whether she knew the person or not, but she had a terrible fear of black cats and electrical storms. If she had known I was walking in one the other day, she would have caned me."

"And are you superstitious too?"

"No, I'm not. It's just funny what she always believed. She thought if a thunderbolt crashed while two people were having a conversation, they had a destiny together."

"A destiny," Julia repeated.

"Yes. But I always believed it was a lot of, to use an old Nebraskan term, 'hogwash'."

* * *

"So you'll be working at school. That's nice," Mrs. Jahns said that evening as she and Julia washed the supper dishes.

"Yup. It sure will save me lots of headaches," Julia said, handing her mother the dish towel. "Not having to rush back home, change into work clothes, then get ready to stand on my feet for four hours. The only bad thing is the twins. They have it in their heads they want to work my same days."

The phone rang and to her disappointment, it was Jenny with her twin sister on the extension.

"That lady Sandee gave us our schedules for work," Jenny announced. "I like her, don't you? She's panic! She knows the inside story on everyone who's ever worked or gone to Raleigh College. Did you know she grew up in the same town as my grandma? Anyway, she gave us your schedule too, as we didn't see you at lunch. Laine and I are working Tuesdays and Thursdays in the psychology department. You're in English. By the way," and her voice went from pleasant to confrontational. "Where were you during lunch? Craig and Lou ate with us. No one had seen you all day."

"Oh I just took a walk," Julia said. "I felt like getting out for a while. The weather's been so nice."

"You never do that. You don't like to walk. Are you mad at us or something?"

"No, not at all. Why do you think I'm mad?"

"I don't know." Jenny decided to leave well enough alone. "Do you want us to drive over tonight and give you your schedule?"

"No, just read it to me. I'll get it from you tomorrow."

She heard Jenny rip open the envelope.

"Let's see, it says Julia Jahns, English Department, Mondays and Fridays, one thirty till four o'clock. Next to the time it says 'flexible'. It's not as many hours as you had at Roote's and it's less money too. But we'll all be saving on gas and car bills."

"Jenny, you haven't told her the big news," Laine said. "Jules, you won't believe what happened to her today!"

"Oh, it's nothing," Jenny said, matter-of-fact. "Just that Craig finally asked me out. We're going to the movies Saturday night!" Her voice became a high-pitched squeal.

"That's great, Jenny," Julia said. "Did he ask you at lunch?"

"Yes, that's why I'm not mad at you for not showing up. Anyway, he and Lou had asked to sit with us. Lou, of course, proceeded to ask where *you* were. I told you he likes you! Then after we ate, Craig asked if I were busy Saturday!"

"I think," Laine said, "that their plan was for Craig to ask Jenny out and then Lou was supposed to chime in and ask Julia out. But since Julia wasn't there, Craig decided to go for it."

"Yeah, Lou did act disappointed to find you missing, Jules," Jenny said. "I think he was looking for you because after lunch I saw him waiting in Professor Hunter's office."

"I wasn't in Professor Hunter's office. Why was he doing that?"

Jenny, not hearing her, continued talking.

"I really think it's meant to be for me and Craig. Isn't he gorgeous? I love guys with blue eyes and dark hair. And he's built. He reminds me of Daddy with his football player physique. Daddy played football all through high school, did I ever tell you that, Jules?"

"Unlike Professor Hunter who looks like the first big wind would blow him over," Laine said, chuckling. "What do you think, Jules? You think you'll go out with Louis? I know he's going to ask you."

Julia hesitated.

"Oh come on!" Jenny said. "The guy's older! Just like you like! You will go out with him, won't you?"

"I don't think so. I mean, I don't know," Julia said.

She tried to think of a plausible excuse.

"He's a nice guy all right but he's more like a friend."

"You say that about all the guys you meet," Jenny cried. "When are you going to stop this? You're going to end up like Aunt Tula. You are so stupid, Julia, it's like you have to be madly in love with someone before you go out with them? Give someone a chance. Lou is so nice. Cute too! And we could tell he is interested."

"And for heaven's sake, he's twenty-six," Laine added. "Isn't that old enough for you?"

"Don't tell me you really like Professor Hunter," Jenny said. "Over someone like Louis? There's no comparison!"

"By the way," Laine said, lowering her voice. "When I saw Sandee for the schedules, she told me she thinks Professor Hunter is a homosexual. She didn't want to say it the other day in front of Julia. But he drinks, smokes and he might go out with men too? I don't know, Julia. Just forget about the whole thing."

"He's not a homosexual," Julia said.

The firmness in her voice surprised her friends.

"And how would *you* know that?" Jenny demanded.

"There are some people who assume all unmarried men are homosexual. It's really unfair. I think Sandee is well, a bit outspoken. And she's wrong."

"And I repeat: how would *you* know that?" Jenny argued. "Sandee must know a lot more than you do. She interacts with the professors all the time. She sees things that go on."

"Maybe she better watch what she says then," Julia said, stunning both herself and the twins with her sharp retort. "Because spreading lies like that might just get her fired."

After she had hung up with the twins, Julia dismissed their words. Aiden Hunter gay? The thought was absurd. She had felt his warmth, his liking for her on just the few occasions they had spoken. Gay men did not care about nineteen-year-old women. They did not ask young ladies out for coffee if they were attracted to men.

"Who was on the phone?" Mrs. Jahns asked as she walked past her daughter, noticing her scowl.

"Nobody worth mentioning," Julia said. She picked up her books from off the kitchen counter and went upstairs to her room. She wanted to be alone and relive every moment she had spent with Aiden Hunter.

CHAPTER FOUR

The little boy watched his mother as she sat in the rocking chair. She was holding his dead brother's blanket, the one embroidered with lambs. She did that a lot. Today he noticed how cold the house seemed. He heard the March wind rattling the windowpane. His mother got up and took something out of the closet. She wrapped George's blanket around it. He followed her down the hall and out to the porch. "Stay here," she told him but he followed her. Her voice scared him. He saw her go into the yard near the shed. He crouched down and put his fingers in his mouth, something he always did when he was nervous. Suddenly a loud bang made him jump. He felt his skin prickle and he stood up, round-eyed, looking at a heap of clothes that was his mother. "Mama, mama," he cried and bent down. He held her hand in his because his mother always loved to hold his hand. That's where his father and uncle found him hours later. They had to pry his little fingers from a hand that was stiff and cool, the wedding band gleaming in the afternoon sun.

Winter days of 1975 eased slowly into spring. March turned cold and nasty, surprising everyone, as if to punish the town for enjoying a mild winter. Julia's days at college were busy. She no longer spent much time in the student lounge for being Aiden's assistant consumed her. As the work-study position continued, she noticed she rarely did any work for the other professor assigned to her.

"Professor Hunter will keep you busy," Sandee Dee had explained, "because he was just elected chair for the entire department."

The first day of the work study, Sandee had walked her to Aiden's office. She made the introductions, unaware Aiden and Julia already knew each other.

"How much time can you put in today?" Aiden asked when Sandee departed. "I have to steal you away from the other professor. If you don't mind, I'd like you to accompany me to the library and help organize some papers."

Aiden took a battered can from under his desk and began watering his many plants. Julia noticed a small vase that stood empty.

"What's usually in there?" she asked.

"Hmmmmm?" Aiden said absent-mindedly. "Oh, that's the vase I keep my dandelions in. By mid-April you will see that it will be full."

"Of dandelions?"

"I'm not sentimental but dandelions cheer me. Don't know why. I suppose it's because they're bright and bloom early. A reminder of better weather ahead. Some see them as mere weeds."

"They are pretty," Julia said. "They're also free for the taking."

"In abundance. I usually pick some right in that field by the parking lot."

He put the watering can under his desk and picked up his briefcase.

"Now, if you're ready, let's continue on to other things."

Julia followed him to Warren Hall. They settled themselves in a small room off the corner of the library. He pulled out a stack of essays and scattered them on the table. As he instructed, she began filing them in manila folders, matching the student's name to the proper folder.

As she did so, Aiden was quiet, chewing on his pen as he graded papers.

"Hmmmm," he murmured several minutes later. "This one's full of reference to scripture."

"What is?" Julia said.

"This paper. Full of Bible verses. This student seems to think God is the cure-all to all modern day problems."

"Well maybe he is," Julia said.

"I'm an apostate of the faith."

He bit the pen so hard it snapped in two.

"That means you once had a faith," Julia responded. Her nervousness about talking to him had evaporated. She was glad he wanted to talk about God.

"Maybe at age five. Religion is a crutch. Anyone who has any sense can see that things happen in our lives that have no rhyme or reason. Evil people flourish while the good man withers – or something to that effect."

"'When the wicked spring as the grass, and when all the workers of iniquity do flourish; it is that they shall be destroyed forever'," Julia said. "I believe it's from Psalms. So the evil man eventually will be destroyed. And evil too."

"Aha," Aiden said, smiling. "So you too are quite pious. And you know the holy book."

"I believe in God," Julia said. "I would believe even if the whole world stopped believing."

She sounded so adamant that Aiden stopped writing and regarded her with amusement.

"You have a determined faith, I see. That is all well and good. It is praiseworthy that you stand on your principles."

Julia blushed.

"Most youth today are heathens," Aiden said. "With their free love and anti-God mantra. Very few set foot inside a church."

"I never liked people who followed the crowd," Julia said. "Even when I was a little girl, I never wanted to be just like everyone else."

"A nonconformist are you then? But you don't confront people. So you're a timid nonconformist."

"I don't like arguments. They bother me. Believe it or not, they make me cry and I hate crying in front of others. That's why I try not to ever put myself into a position where I'll get upset in public."

"If such is the case, I have no doubt those friends of yours remain the nemesis in your life. They look like such disagreeable young women. Are they churchgoers as well?"

"Yes, they both go to church."

"It's enough to make one remain an agnostic."

"Well, going to church doesn't make you a believer any more than going into a garage makes you a car."

"Interesting analogy. You have shed a new light on faith but I still remain a scoffer."

"But why?"

"Nothing can be proven. Nothing in the end makes sense."

"You're wrong. You can't scientifically prove love but when you feel it, you know it exists."

He looked at her with a wry smile.

"That's not love, hmmmmm? That may be hormones or what have you. But what exactly is 'true love'? The kind they write about. Does not exist. Unless maybe love of self. Ah, yes, the truest love of them all."

"That sounds so cynical."

"Come back to see me when you're forty-five and we'll go into it further, Miss Jahns."

His smile disappeared and he pulled out a cigarette. His black reading glasses slipped down his nose and he absent-mindedly adjusted them. Julia studied him in fascination.

I wonder if that means he's forty-five!

"I was nineteen once," he said, more to himself than to her. "I was once in Arcadia."

His eyes looked distant. He was remembering a past time and reliving a memory she could not share.

"Arcadia," Julia echoed, feeling a twinge of jealousy.

"Hmmmmm, but it didn't last."

He sighed and went back to reading the essay. Julia did the rest of her work in silence, not wanting to disturb his concentration. The remainder of their time together went quickly by.

"I must get going."

Aiden rose to his feet, shoving papers back into his briefcase.

"You can finish the rest of the filing next time."

His tone made Julia feel awkward. The friendly warmth of his voice had dissipated.

"I'll put them back in your office," she said.

"Very well. I shall see you then."

And he left her, scurrying across the library back into the main building through the heavy glass doors.

* * *

The following week, Julia walked alone to the auditorium where her psychology class was being held. The instructor planned to combine several of his classes to hear a guest speaker. Julia had not seen the twins for several days as they had skipped Aiden Hunter's class and had not called her over the weekend. She was hoping to avoid them awhile longer as she was enjoying the drama-free atmosphere.

As she approached the last row of seats, she caught sight of Jenny and Laine, their backs to her. Craig McCrory and his friend Louis Merlowe were standing alongside them. A small partition separated the group from Julia so she could eavesdrop without being seen.

"Julia's unique," Laine was saying. "We do love her but she's, well.….. different."

"I think you're being too diplomatic," Craig said. "She likes the loons 'cause she's a loon. I had Hunter last year. He's totally unwrapped."

"Hey now, not really nice to talk about someone who's not here," Louis said. "And this was the girl I heard so much about?"

"You've only heard half of it," Jenny said. "Julia deserves to be talked about because she ignores everything we say. Who would have thought she'd really like the guy?"

"Wait," Louis said. "Who are we talking about? Her professor?"

"Yes, Hunter," Jenny said. "She likes him! And not like you think. She like-likes him! I mean, look at him. He's so old. And you know what I think? He looks a bit like her dad when her dad was young. I saw a picture of Julia's father once. Her mom had a photo of him on the wall."

"He looked like Hunter?" Craig said.

"Not identical to him but, yeah. Very similar. Same build and dark hair. And that very white skin."

"Well that explains it," Louis said, trying to dismiss the conversation. "A father figure. Case closed."

"She's been acting like a real pain lately," Jenny continued. "And it's got to stop. She hasn't done anything with us or with Pammy or Mary Lou over the last few weekends. I know she isn't babysitting her brothers anymore because her mom told our mom they've been going to their aunt's. Maybe we should tell Mrs. Jahns what's going on with her."

"Tell her mother what?" Laine said. "It's not like she's dating him. Besides, we both were the ones to tell her to take his class when she didn't need the class. We pushed her into it."

"Who would've thought she'd really go for him?" Jenny said. "Telling her about him was more of a joke. I honestly didn't think it would turn into anything serious. All her old man crushes were always just that --- stupid crushes. But now I'm thinking, maybe she's really dating him. Have you seen or heard from her? I thinks she spends too much time around him. And she never comments on how she likes working for him. I also notice how he watches her in class. I don't think she's aware of it. Who knows what he's up to? He could be a pervert."

Craig threw back his head and laughed. Before anything more could be said, Julia backed away. She slipped out the side door and into the hall. Better to skip the class than to show her hurt and betrayal.

Suddenly feeling sick, Julia decided to walk past Aiden's office to see if he were there. Situated in the corner of a small hallway, he had chosen it for the privacy it afforded him. She was disappointed to find his door shut. A closed door meant he was either gone for the day or at a meeting. The combination of her friends' criticisms and Aiden's unavailability wreaked havoc with her fragile emotions. Thinking she was alone, she buried her face in her hands and wept. She was angry with herself for crying but felt burdened by an overwhelming sense of aloneness. She could not stop the tears.

They think I'm a freak! The whole school will hate me. Everyone hates me. I wish I could die!

Seconds later, Aiden's office door swung open. A husky man in his early forties, with dark red hair, stood before her. He was dressed in a navy blue three-piece suit, a pair of gold bifocals hanging from a chain around his neck. The stranger was as surprised to see her as she was to see him. His black eyes squinted, first in alarm, then compassion.

"Excuse me, miss," he said. "Is something wrong?"

The sound of a sympathetic voice made Julia's weeping intensify.

"There, there," the man said, patting her arm. "Let's go in here."

He walked Julia into Aiden's office, closing the door behind them. Leading her over the arm chair, he made her sit down and placed her pocketbook on the floor.

"Please, tell me what's wrong," he said as she fumbled in her pocket for a tissue. "Here, let me."

He handed her a Kleenex box from Aiden's desk.

"Thank you," Julia said, her voice muffled in the tissue.

"Not at all," the man replied. He gave her some time to collect herself then stretched out his hand.

"My name is Guenther Hunter," he said "and I'm pleased to make your acquaintance, Miss, Miss?"

"Jahns," she said shaking his hand. "Julia Jahns."

"Well Julia," Guenther Hunter said, smiling. "I hope whatever is distressing you is soon dispensed with. I have five children of my own, my oldest daughter looking to be about your age. I would hate to think of her crying alone in some corner at school."

"Your last name is Hunter?"

Julia sniffed, wiping her eyes one last time, feeling better at the sound of the familiar name.

"Are you related to my professor?"

"Aiden Hunter? Why yes, I'm his brother. He has no idea I'm here. I had to fly to New York yesterday to see an old friend and I thought I'd pop over to Jersey and surprise him. I guess the surprise is on me. Aiden is missing."

Julia looked closely at Guenther Hunter. The only similarity between Aiden and his brother was the color of their eyes. What the second Mr. Hunter lacked in classic good looks, he made up for in personality. Of the two siblings, Guenther was the extrovert. He had a broad and cheerful smile; his eyes twinkled when he spoke. His skin was darker than Aiden's, with a sprinkling of freckles on his hands and face.

"Were you waiting to see Aiden as well?" Guenther asked.

"Not exactly. I mean, I work for him part-time."

"I was going to ask one of the secretaries when he'd be returning. I guess I arrived at their lunch hour."

Guenther glanced at his watch.

"I wanted to take him to lunch. Of course I have no idea what his schedule is. He could be back at his apartment for all I am aware. Did you say you work for him? Are you a secretary?"

"In a way. I'm a student here but I assist him and another English teacher with clerical duties. It's a work study program our school offers. And I don't know his schedule for today. It's not my usual day to work with him. Since he's not here, I better be going."

"Oh, I see. Well, Miss Jahns, it was so very nice meeting you. I hope the rest of your day goes better than your last half hour."

Guenther once again shook her hand, then opened the door for her.

"I will tell Aiden that we met," he said. "I think I will hang around a bit in hopes of catching him."

Julia spent the rest of that day sitting on a park bench near her house. She tried to read a book but her mind wandered. Feeling out of sorts, she did not want to go home, yet she did not want to return to campus. She was depressed Aiden had not been there when she wanted to see him. Restless and unhappy, she wished she could leave her body and fly away. Like a bird. She watched a blue jay in a nearby tree take flight, disappearing from view until it was just a dark speck. She was sick of her friends and wanted to rid herself of them forever.

What's wrong with me, she thought. *Why don't I want to go out with a guy like Louis Merlowe? He's definitely good looking. Any other girl would grab him up. He doesn't interest me in the least. And why am I lonely even when I'm with people my own age in school? Why do I feel like I am always on the outside looking in?*

She looked up into the sky, tears welling in her eyes.

Oh God, I hate my life. I wish my dad was around. I wish I didn't have to worry about money all the time. I wish my mom could be home more. And I really wish I could make Professor Hunter want me. Maybe even marry me!

Her thoughts became her prayers. Julia believed Aiden Hunter's love would fill up the void in her heart. If only God would grant her that one request, that Aiden would love her, she knew life would be perfect. She was certain she would never feel lonely again.

The following day Julia went home for lunch but returned to Raleigh in time for her next class. The phone had rung several times while she ate, but she did not answer it. She was afraid the callers were the twins checking up on her. Walking from the parking lot to the college building, Julia noticed Sandee Dee getting out of her car. Sandee saw her and waved.

"Hey, luv, how's the romance going?" she said when she had caught up to Julia. "How's the job with Mr. Insipid? Bored yet?"

"No, I like the job."

"Your friends Frick and Frack are worried about you."

"Frick and Frack can mind their own business," Julia said, frowning. "But please don't tell them I said that."

"Mum's the word. I think you have two friends who need to focus more on themselves. They were giving me the third degree about Dr. Hunter."

"I know. And I know what they're like. They told me you said he's a homosexual."

"Look," Sandee said, her grin disappearing. "I know you think I'm just an old lady and who listens to old ladies? But I've worked here twenty years. Dr. Hunter has been here ten. The rumor mill always put out that he's queer. That he left a teaching position in Michigan over a love affair with a male colleague that went sour. Now," Sandee paused when she saw Julia's eyes widen, "they're just rumors. Nothing to back them up and no one has ever told me they'd actually seen Hunter do anything that wasn't kosher. He keeps to himself. But the scuttlebutt amongst the staff is that he's gay."

Julia stiffened.

"You know I don't believe that."

"I can see you don't," Sandee said, her smile returning. "Who knows for sure, luv? Life is short. Why let it worry you. Maybe he's just introverted or, you know what they say about the real bookworm types, he's a bit anti-social.

I just figured he's queer for the simple reason he never gave me a second look. Most of the male teachers here have propositioned me at least once!"

Sandee's laughter rang out but Julia did not respond in kind. She was now convinced that Sandee, for all her motherly ways, was trouble.

* * *

The next time she saw the twins, Julia said very little. They still sat beside her in Aiden's class but this time they ignored her, engrossed in a private conversation. Jenny looked as if she were near tears. They darted out of class when it was over, not waiting for her. Aiden was busy talking to a student but when he saw that she about to leave, he ended his conversation.

"Miss Jahns, before you go," he said. "Can I see you for a moment?"

He waited until the class emptied and shut the door.

"I don't want to keep you," he said. "But I hear you met my brother."

"Yes, we talked for a few minutes."

"Hmmmm, well it appears he's in town for a week. He's having lunch with me Friday. I know that's when I have you working with me and I'd like to ask if you can do me a favor."

"Yes?"

"Please don't feel you have to agree to this."

It seemed as if Aiden were struggling to get the words out.

"As I say, he's eating with me Friday. Our relationship is not good. Not that it is bad, but it's, well, it's strained. I told him we can eat in the cafeteria here on campus and he wasn't happy about that. He wants to wine and dine me at a restaurant. But, well, it's just more comfortable when I'm surrounded by students and faculty. My natural setting, so to speak."

Julia nodded, wondering where this was going.

"What I mean to say, if I may be so bold, is that I'd like you to join us. Have lunch with us. Since you have already met him, and I don't want to be alone with him, it would be doing me a favor. More than you know."

Julia paused. *Eat with Aiden Hunter and his brother? Why it's like he's wanting me to meet his family!* Her heart began pounding so violently she thought it was audible.

"It's awkward," Aiden continued. "Conversation between us, that is. Our lives are so very different. Again, you don't have to. I'm asking you only if you'd be so gracious."

"Okay," Julia replied. She tried not to blush but she felt her face get hot.

"Our relationship is not close," Aiden continued, not noticing her discomfort. "There's a lot of loose ends from the past we have up to now ignored. I'd rather not go into it but it's, well, the whole thing is difficult."

He paused.

"I guess I'm not asking you as a teacher asking a student. Rather, I am asking you as a friend. So don't feel you have to come."

"No, I will come."

She was touched by his words. He considered her his friend. He cared about her enough to call her his friend! If Sandee was right and Aiden had always kept to himself, this was indeed an answer to her prayers.

Thank you, God, Julia prayed. *Thank you so much.*

She returned to the student lounge, ecstatic. In her daydreams, she saw herself walking beside Aiden, part of his life, part of his family. Being with him and talking to him every day! Sharing her thoughts with him. The lonely pit in her stomach felt like it had melted away. And this Friday, in just a few more days, she was going to eat with him. And be with his brother! Not long ago she had gone for coffee with him! Today he called her *his friend!* Could life get any better?

It was odd but Julia did not feel romantic when she was actually with Aiden Hunter. She was happy and content in his presence, but there were no sparks. It was later, when she was alone, that she felt a mesmerizing desire for him. Since she had never been in love or had a relationship with a man, she thought her feelings were totally normal. *This is love,* she thought. *It has to be the love I've always wanted. He makes me so happy. I could spend all day with him.* Could it be he was feeling the same way too?

As she neared the couch where she normally sat, Julia spotted Pammy with the twins. Her mind snapped back to reality. Pam held a tissue to her face and was blowing her nose. Julia was about to walk the other way when she heard Jenny's voice.

"Stop it! Kevin is not worth it," Jenny said. "Stop crying. No guy is worth it."

"Shhhh," Laine admonished. "Lower your voice."

"I'm not letting Pam cry like this," Jenny said. "She's got to stop!"

Julia could not hear Pammy's response but she saw her lower her head.

"Kevin isn't in our league," Jenny said. "You knew this was going to happen. Guys like him don't date girls like us. I warned you, Pam. For God's sake you're getting as stupid as Julia!"

Laine pulled on Pam's arm and led her away. Jenny was left standing alone. The latter turned around and suddenly noticed Julia, but before she could say anything, Julia walked quickly away. Whatever fireworks Jenny was creating, Julia did not want to be burned.

* * *

Friday came. Julia stood in Aiden's office looking around at his messy bookshelves. It was late morning. She had been sent to him with pamphlets from another professor who was trying to coax him into joining yet another committee.

"Work, work, it never ends," Aiden mumbled as he took the package from her. "Thank you for these." And he threw it on a pile of unopened mail.

Julia wondered if he was going to mention their lunch date with his brother. He was muttering to himself, moving papers from his desk and looking under folders.

"Can I help you with anything?" Julia said.

"Lost my wallet," Aiden said. "Oh, well, it shall turn up eventually."

"I really should straighten out your bookshelves one of these days," Julia said, wrinkling her nose at the mess. "I don't know how you can find any of your things with everything so cluttered."

Aiden was now opening his desk drawers, still searching for the wallet.

"Yes it is rather unsightly."

Julia noticed a small cardboard picture frame lying on the floor that had fallen from a shelf. Curious, she picked it up. It contained a black and white photo, very battered and yellowing, obviously taken years ago. She stared at the photo for a few moments, frozen. The face in the picture looking back at her was the face of a woman not much older than herself. The word "ADA" was penciled in the corner of the peeling paper frame.

"What's that?" Aiden said, looking over to where she stood, wallet now in hand. "I found my wallet and --- what is that you've got?"

Julia did not hear him. She was completely engrossed in the photograph.

My goodness, she thought, *this woman looks enough like me to be my twin sister!*

"What have you got there?" Aiden repeated. He walked over to Julia who held the tiny frame cupped in her two hands.

"It was on the floor, it must have fallen," Julia said. "I picked it up. Who is this?"

Aiden took the photo from her and studied it, his expression softening. "Ada, Ada," he whispered.

"Ada?" Julia said. "Who is she?"

"It's the picture of an angel," he said. "It's my mother."

* * *

An hour later, Julia and Aiden sat in the cafeteria at Raleigh College, sharing a table with Guenther Hunter. Julia had looked forward to this moment but now that it was here, she felt ill at ease. It was obvious that the two brothers were not at all close. Aiden looked stiff and disinterested. Guenther, to his credit, tried to reach out to his sibling. He talked about his five children, his busy practice, and his soon-to-be-finalized divorce. He praised his wife for her amiability throughout their separation and raved about his offspring. He spoke about his hometown in Nebraska and how he enjoyed raising his children there. He tried to engage Aiden but was unsuccessful. Aiden smiled and nodded at the appropriate moments but his responses were chilly. Julia sipped her coffee slowly, trying to make it last so that she had something to do. She felt like a fifth wheel, obviously just a prop for Aiden, and she sensed Guenther's puzzlement as to her presence.

"This is my assistant, Miss Jahns, my work study student," Aiden had told him. "I hope you don't mind her dining with us. She's working with me today and she skipped lunch to run an errand for me earlier."

The white lie was not lost on Julia.

Guenther had cleared his throat, sensing Julia's discomfort.

"No, no, not at all," he had said. "It's nice to see you again, Miss Jahns."

Julia nodded. As Guenther made small talk, she looked around the cafeteria to see if anyone she knew was noticing the three of them.

"Now Aiden," Guenther said later, turning to his brother as they finished their lunch. "I'm not going to be here long. But I was hoping you'd show me around New York. I hear you know the city pretty well."

"Why do you say that?" Aiden said, his tone sharp. Julia wondered why the question annoyed him.

"Didn't mean to upset you," Guenther said, holding up his hand as if to shield himself from Aiden's vitriol. "You told me you chose your apartment in Tilletson so you could be a few miles from the Big Apple. I take it that you frequent New York quite often."

Julia was surprised to hear where Aiden lived. Up to this point, she had no idea where his apartment was located. Tilletson was seedy. She couldn't imagine why Aiden would choose to live there. Unless, of course, he preferred an area where rents were low. *Was Aiden poor?* Because Tilletson was a city that had seen much better days.

"I think Julia is done with her coffee and would no doubt like to leave the two of us," Guenther said, smiling at her. "If you will walk me to my car, Aiden, perhaps we can arrange a time to meet later tonight. Dinner perhaps? I hear there are good restaurants in Tilletson."

If you want to dine carrying a gun, Julia thought. *What a dump!*

She was relieved Guenther was dismissing her. Her discomfort escalating, her new desire was to be alone with her thoughts.

Aiden stared into his cup, dunking the teabag up and down.

"I'm sure we are keeping you from your friends," Guenther said as Julia gathered her books to leave. "Or a boyfriend or two."

"I do have a class soon," she said.

Guenther nodded but Aiden said nothing. Julia walked out of the room feeling his eyes on her back.

As soon as she was gone, Guenther's mood changed. His smile disappeared and he regarded his brother with disgust.

"And what was that all about?" he said.

"What do you mean?"

"Bringing that young girl with you."

Aiden did not answer.

"Never mind. Let us go back to your office where we can speak more privately."

Carrying his mug of tea, Aiden followed his brother out of the cafeteria.

"I'm not here to start an argument with you," Guenther said after closing the office door. "Though you treat me like an outlaw. I'm here because time is marching on, we're getting older. We should call it a truce."

"You're here because your wife is gone and now you suddenly feel a fraternal tug at your heart," Aiden said.

He sat behind his desk, Guenther in the armchair in front of him.

"Such sarcasm, Aiden," Guenther sighed. "I'd have been here for visits years ago but you were so angry and I never thought you'd want to see me. I'm not pushing myself on anyone. It was also hard getting away from a busy practice and trying to raise five kids. You never even ask about my kids. They have an uncle who is a complete stranger."

Aiden stirred his tea, his eyes down.

"You also never called to say you were ill," Guenther continued. "I spoke to your doctor after I got the call from the hospital. He said you were near death when your landlord found you. If it weren't for that landlord, God bless his soul, you'd be dead right now and I'd be visiting a tombstone. The doctor told me your blood alcohol level was --- my God, why are you drinking so much? And how did you explain the whole thing to the college?"

"My doctor told them it was a viral infection," Aiden said, his face expressionless. "It was nobody's business."

"I've never held anything against you, Aiden. I know Father mistreated you and favored me. There's nothing I can do about that. I admit I wasn't the best of brothers when we were young. I'm also sorry Father funded my education but made you work. Life isn't fair sometimes and I don't know why Father was the way he was. He's been gone ten years, can't we forget about it?"

Aiden did not reply.

"Father never accepted you and Joseph." Guenther lowered his voice to a near whisper. "I know that was part of why he was so angry with you. But I don't want to rehash all that now."

"Joseph's been dead twenty years," Aiden said, his voice shaking. "How ironic he died a decade before the old man. Father, who wasn't supposed to last more than a month with cancer, outlived Joseph by ten years. It's unfathomable. Joseph was so pure of heart, so sweet. Father was a bitter and ugly human being."

"I will never forget hearing about the car accident," Guenther said, shaking his head. "And I will never forget where I was. Joseph was my best friend all through childhood, remember. I know you loved him but I did too. Not in the same way, of course, but I loved him as a brother. He tutored me in English all through high school. In fact, I credit him for getting me into college. He was a fine young man, a terrific writer. So much potential! And I never held it against either of you for your ….. uh, the relationship you shared. Shocked maybe that he was, well, that he was that way. But things are what they are. And I blame myself for the accident. I was supposed to pick him up that day, he wasn't feeling well. Who knows, maybe if I hadn't.…" His voice trailed off and both men were silent, lost in thought. Guenther saw Aiden's face soften. Then it changed and his black eyes turned icy.

"It's neither here nor there," Aiden said. "You did nothing wrong. A drunk driver hit him. It was long ago. Now nothing really matters. He's gone. Your sorrow, my sorrow, all for naught."

"I cried many tears over that death," Guenther said.

"If tears could bring him back, my tears alone would have resurrected him," Aiden replied. "I'm sure our father was delighted that he was dead. Problem solved, Father thought. My oldest son can now be normal. Marry and have children."

"I don't know what Father was thinking," Guenther said. "I don't pretend I can climb into someone's mind. But this is all the past. You and I, we are alive. We are brothers. We need to mend our fences and start being kind to each other."

Aiden did not respond.

"Okay then, I see you're not ready to engage in a friendly dialogue," Guenther said, realizing his brother's wooden response was not softening. "Not to pick a fight, but let me change the subject. I'd like to know why you brought that student to lunch today. I found it insulting. I ask to see you and you bring someone with you. As if to say, let's not have a conversation."

"She's a nice young lady and she missed her lunch," Aiden lied. "Because I have her running around for me doing my chores. No other reason than that, I assure you."

"All right, I just thought it odd. She's what, eighteen years old?"

"That's none of your business. I'm not interested in discussing her."

"Okay, Aiden, I was just curious. She reminded me of my Shelley. Do you even remember my daughter? My first born. And you were one of the first to hold her when we brought her home from the hospital. We always said Shelley looked so much like ---"

"I do remember Shelley. And Miss Jahns looks nothing like her. My student is a very good worker and a blossoming writer. I felt guilty at her having to skip her lunch today."

"Very well," Guenther replied. "Whatever you say, Aiden. If you don't mind, I shall take my leave. If you'd be so kind as to walk me to my car."

And the two men left the room.

CHAPTER FIVE

Not again. The young father rolled out of bed, awakened by the sounds of his son's high-pitched shrieks. Another bad dream. It had been like this for months, the child screaming in terror in the middle of the night. The father was at his wit's end. Walking toward the boy's room, he rubbed his eyes, again feeling overwhelmed and helpless. Sticking his head into the room, he saw his younger son in peaceful slumber in the twin bed, undisturbed by the commotion. But the older boy, his black hair plastered to his head in sweat, sat up, sobbing, holding out his arms to his father. The man stood there, looking at the child. Why couldn't he comfort his own son? Something inside urged him to pick the child up and cuddle him, tell him things were all right. After all, he was not even six years old. Yet another part of the man was disgusted. This was no way for a male child to act. The boy had annoyed him in the past with his sissified ways, his clinginess, his over-sensitivity. He never felt comfortable with this son, had always felt this was his wife's child and Guenther more his own. But now his wife was dead and he was alone, father to both sons. He stood in the doorway, hesitant, watching his little boy. "Go to sleep now, your brother's nearby. Go to sleep. You're a big boy now, you have to stop crying. Go to sleep." He did not go near him, just continued to repeat the same refrain, "Go to sleep now. That's enough. You're a big boy. Stop crying."

Early one morning in late March, Julia stood by the cafeteria door, fumbling in her purse for a dollar. Suddenly hungry, she wanted to buy a roll and a hot tea. Her next class started in fifteen minutes and she did not want to be late. Always conscientious of being on time, she was even more so when the class was Aiden's.

Maybe she should bring a tea to Professor Hunter, too, she thought, fishing for another dollar bill. No, that wouldn't look right. She paused, remembering the last time she had been with Aiden, helping him sort books in his office. That day she had noticed he was watching her with a look she had never seen before. He was studying her and his eyes looked engaged. Like this time he was really seeing her. She had never had an older man look at her like that before. Almost like he was hungry. *Oh, but that's silly,* she thought, suddenly embarrassed at her own inner narrative. Aiden Hunter at this point certainly liked her and enjoyed talking to her but *wanting* her? Ridiculous.

Still, it made her heart suddenly beat faster. *Could it be?* Was it possible that he could fall in love with her?

The thought was so intriguing that she stood still, forgetting her search for money, forgetting her hunger pangs. She could visualize his black eyes gazing into her own, telling her he loved her. She could see ---

"Hey look what the wind blew in."

A loud male voice interrupted her daydream.

Julia woke up to see Craig McCrory, Jenny close by his side, grinning at her. He was a tall, good looking youth with dark brown hair and deep set blue eyes fringed with long eyelashes. Julia knew the type. A boy in love with himself who thought every female was crazy about him.

Jenny grabbed Craig's arm possessively and shot Julia a smug look.

"Well, hello there, Julia. I hear so much about you but you've been a stranger in these parts," Craig said. "We never see you around. Your friend here has been asking about you."

He patted the top of Jenny's head.

What is she, a dog? Julia thought.

"I guess the work study's been keeping you busy," Jenny said. "You've met Craig before, haven't you Jules?"

"Yes," Julia said. "Nice to see you again."

"Can I buy you girls a coffee?" Craig said. "Jenny and I are going to do some studying in here before my nine thirty class."

"Actually I was just going to buy a snack and then leave," Julia said. "We do have that eight o'clock English Lit class, Jenny."

"Oh for God's sake, that horribly boring class with that freak," Jenny cried. "You can go without me, Jules. I'm cutting. I'm in no mood to listen to him drone on and on about nothing."

"Is that the class with your boyfriend?" Craig said to Julia with a wink. "I hear you go for the older men but wow, he's gotta be pushing fifty."

"He's not my boyfriend," Julia said.

"Well you're sure with him an awful lot," Jenny said. "I never see you working with that other teacher you were assigned to."

"The rumors are gonna fly," Craig said, grabbing a donut off a table that someone had left behind. He stuffed it into his mouth saying, "Not that we guys gossip. We just hear it from our ladies."

Crumbs spilled out of his mouth as he talked. Jenny smiled up at him with a look that made Julia wince.

She's such a dip, Julia thought. *I'd never go out with a boorish dumb-dumb like Craig McCrory. Where is her pride?*

"Hey, before you go," Craig said, wiping his mouth with the back of his sleeve. "You met my friend Lou? He's a cool dude. He might be just your type, being an older guy and all. We should double date one night, you and Lou, me and Jenny."

"I --- I --- maybe," Julia said. "I'm not sure. I do have to go."

Before Craig could continue, she quickly left, walking as fast as she could down the hallway, worried the two of them would follow her.

"Hunter's a homo!" she heard Jenny holler out.

Julia was glad to be in Aiden's class without the twins. Laine hadn't shown up either. The class ended five minutes later than usual that day. Aiden had been tardy arriving and wanted to make up the time. Usually he rushed out of the room before the first student had packed up, but today he lingered. He sat atop his desk, watching Julia. She noticed it and made sure she was the last pupil remaining. She fussed with her books until the two of them were alone.

"I know you might be busy," Aiden said. "But tonight I'm participating in a debate in Warren Hall with Professor Riggs. We need someone to work the tape recorder."

"Oh?"

"You see, it's a debate on Beowulf and Grendel and the topic of good versus evil. Professor Riggs suggested we tape the event. We're going to use it for a promotional film for the college. He asked me to find a student to work the tape recorder. Would you like to assist us?"

"When is it?"

She felt her face get warm. Aiden looked at her with a mixture of shyness and affection.

"Tonight at six. I usually take the train home right after my later class but as I have to be back by five thirty or so, I decided to just stay put. Is six too late for you?"

"No, now that I have my own car, it's fine," Julia replied, inwardly thanking Ned and the Lord for her means of transportation. "I can go home for a while and be back at six with no problem."

"I thank you so very much," Aiden said. He looked relieved. "Be at Warren Hall a few minutes before six. You'll sit in the front row and we'll have the recorder ready."

"Okay."

They looked at each other. At that moment it felt as if an electrical current passed between them. It was a physical sensation that caused Julia to take a deep breath. Aiden Hunter must have felt it too for she saw his hands tremble as he picked up his book and left the room.

* * *

That evening, Julia rushed through her homework, anxious to return to Raleigh. She did not mention her plans to her mother, who was busy getting ready for work. Her thoughts were so caught up in romantic fancyings that she barely heard her mother giving her last minute instructions.

"I've dropped your brothers off at Aunt Margie's," Mrs. Jahns said. "There's dinner on the stove. Sorry but it's mac and cheese again. I should be home by eleven. Julia, are you listening?"

"What? Yes. Are the boys coming home with Aunt Margie?"

"She's bringing them home around nine thirty. I know it's a school night but they've stayed up that late before. It's so nice going to work, knowing my sister is watching the boys and I have gem for a daughter. Never have to worry about my girl! I told Clara Murden today that my Jules is truly a jewel. Goes to her room, studies, goes to bed. I think Clara is very concerned about Jenny these days."

"Oh, and why is that?"

"She said Jenny went out with a boy and didn't get home till after three in the morning. Clara was beside herself. What's gotten into those twins lately?"

"I don't know."

"Maybe what I told you before was right. Maybe you need to find yourself some new best friends."

After her mother left, Julia went to her room to feed her birds. She was lost in a reverie, dreaming about Aiden. Her imaginings took her no further than his dark eyes staring deeply into her own or his arm draped around her shoulders. The mental pictures of his love enveloping her were, to her nineteen-year-old heart, more satisfying than his actual physical presence.

The phone rang and annoyed, she picked it up.

Always someone to bother me, she thought. *I hope it isn't Jenny!*

"It's me, Laine," said the voice on the other line. "Look, I know you're mad at us but Jenny's got a big problem."

"I'm not mad at you," Julia said.

"Don't lie. We know you are. You haven't called and Jenny told me you stomped out of the room when she was talking to you."

"I've been busy."

"I just wanted to tell you Jenny is really upset. Not over you leaving the cafeteria although it was rude. But you never asked her about her date with Craig. In fact, they've had a few dates since then. But even that's not what she's upset about."

Maybe because I don't care.

"Anyway," Laine continued, not waiting for a response, "Jenny thinks she might be pregnant. She's late and she's never late. Never."

"What?" Julia snapped to attention. "She *slept* with that guy?"

"What do you think, stupid? Of course she did. You know how nuts she's been over him. She did it with him the first time they went out. Anyway first she thought she was definitely pregnant. Then she thought she wasn't. Late this afternoon she called Craig to tell him it might be a false alarm and he acted real nasty. Like he insinuated it's *her* problem! Now she's back to thinking she is pregnant. I made her a doctor appointment, she is going into hysterics."

"Did she tell your mom?"

"No. Not till we know for sure. I think she'll tell our dad first."

Julia paused. *How idiotic could Jenny be! Running after a guy who obviously didn't like her that much then sleeping with him on the first date! What a fool!*

"Well I sure hope she's not pregnant. I hope it's just nerves."

"So do I," Laine said. "She's worried about my mom but it's my dad who's going to kill her."

Julia was quiet. Laine's tone suddenly changed.

"Speaking of stupidity, I guess you're still interested in that old man professor? Jenny and I decided to drop his class. We're taking English Lit with Professor Varnerum."

"Suit yourself," Julia replied. "And tell Jenny I wish her luck."

* * *

Aiden Hunter glanced at his watch and began piling notebooks on his desk. He had exactly one hour before he had to meet Ashley Riggs and go over the dialog for their debate. Once again, he had misplaced his notes. A dying bulb inside the lamp he kept on his credenza flickered, annoying him. Deep in thought, he did not notice a figure standing in the doorway until that person gently cleared their throat.

"Yes?" Aiden said, squinting in the dimly lit room. "Who's there?"

"Why don't you just turn on the light?" the figure said softly. "My, my, you've always been in the dark about things, haven't you Aiden?"

Sudden anxiety engulfed Aiden and he bent down to retrieve his briefcase.

"I'm sorry but I don't have time for you now," he said. "I have an event to attend and I'm running late. Please come back another time."

He turned toward the figure but to his relief, noticed he was alone.

* * *

Julia drove back to Raleigh for the debate and promptly forgot about the conversation with Laine. Someone as brainless as Jenny Murden did not deserve anyone's sympathy. Julia always believed people who could not control their basic instincts deserved what they got. And to give up your virginity for a conceited nineteen-year-old jock? Why it was the most insane thing Jenny had ever done!

The evening of the debate began uneventfully. An oversized tape recorder in the auditorium resided on a stand in front of the first row of seats where Julia sat. The microphone was hooked up to a wooden rod so that it could pick up both speakers' voices. Julia turned the tape recorder on when Professor Riggs nodded to her, then made sure the mic stayed in place.

Professor Riggs began the debate, reading from a script and speaking in a fake English accent. Aiden would respond in kind, also sounding like an Englishman. They did several retakes before they decided that the finished product was perfect. At seven fifteen, the debate over, Julia turned the machine off. *Not much to that job*, she thought. A few students had wandered into the room to see what was going on. Another English professor had shown up, operating a movie camera. Julia wondered if the taped version were to be added to the film. *Pretty dull viewing*, she thought. Neither debater had sounded British nor had their "argument" appeared convincing. It seemed to be more of an entertainment to the two debaters themselves.

A few moments later, Professor Riggs stretched out his hand to thank Julia for her help. As people filed out of the room, she went inside the cloakroom to retrieve her pocketbook. That's when she heard Aiden call out to her.

"Don't leave just yet."

She turned to see him grab his jacket off a chair.

"I want to walk you to your automobile. I will be right back."

She wanted to protest that walking to the parking lot at night did not frighten her but he had hurried away. Five minutes later he reappeared. By now, the building was vacant. As he stood beside her, she thought she detected the scent of alcohol. *Or maybe it's just his cologne*, she thought. Whatever it was, she hadn't smelled it earlier.

"You didn't have to take time to walk me to my car," Julia said as they made their way across the room and into the hallway. "The lot is well lit."

"Rubbish, it's dark out, you never know," Aiden said. "It's the least I can do after you came tonight. And after enduring lunch with my brother."

He held the door open for her and she walked out into the fresh air. The March night was cold and crisp. Brilliant starts lit up an inky sky. The moon was full. Julia looked up to admire the view.

Aiden was nervous as he fumbled with his jacket.

"It's so beautiful out," Julia said as they began to walk.

"Yes it is."

He paused, then said:

"Almost as beautiful as you."

His words so startled her that she dropped her purse.

"Forgive me," Aiden said, bending over to pick it up, "but that statement just popped out of me."

He looked up into the sky and reached for her hand. To her astonishment, he intertwined his fingers through hers.

What is he doing! With a pounding heart, she stood still, transfixed in shock. Then paralyzing shyness enfolded her like a blanket and she felt like she was smothering. She could not catch her breath.

"When I was younger," Aiden said, oblivious to her reaction. "I sometimes felt that this is what heaven will be like. A vast abyss, looking like the view of the sky tonight. As breathtaking as a painting. A place where we would have the answer to all our yearnings. But since I no longer believe in heaven, I can now just admire nature's dazzling display. I am resigned to the fact that sometimes yearnings will never be fulfilled."

"Aren't you happy?" Julia asked when she was able to speak.

"Man is never happy," Aiden shrugged. "Who knows the reason?"

He kept his hand in hers and they resumed their walk.

"God is the only one who can understand our yearnings," she replied.

Julia felt awkward, not knowing if she should pull her hand away or tighten her grip. She wondered when he would release her, part of her hoping he would, but part of her wanting him to hold on.

"As I told you, I don't believe in God. But to be honest, I wish I did. To think this is all there is, well...."

"That's a depressing thought," Julia responded, glad the topic was on spirituality. "Because we know we are all going to die. I always realized no matter how long I may live, someday I am going to cease to exist. No one can escape it."

"It might be reassuring to you that I will die ahead of you," he said with a smile. "Then you can sit smugly in your rocking chair and think 'Now Aiden Hunter knows I'm right. There is a heaven and he, poor soul, is rotting in hell.'"

"That's an awful thing to say!" Julia exclaimed, so horrified at the thought of hellfire that she forgot her timidity. "If you really believed in hell, and there is one for sure, you would never make jokes!"

"Calm down," Aiden said. "My, my, you're so intense."

He released her hand and motioned to a bench that abutted the parking lot. "Sit down."

She obeyed, pulling her jacket tighter around her. The night air was cold and she felt a chill. Aiden sat beside her and lit a cigarette. After taking several puffs, he took hold of her hand and put it in his coat pocket.

"I don't take the subject of hell lightly," Julia said. "Didn't you ever worry about death when you were in the hospital? Didn't eternity and where you were headed occur to you at all? If that had been me, that would have been my first thought."

"That's because you are so impassioned," Aiden said. "I like that about you."

"No, it's because I'm realistic."

He took a long drag on his cigarette.

"I actually did think about dying when I was so ill. But I didn't care if I died. Not at all. In fact, I was hoping to die."

His face was grim, his lips set in a hard line. She wanted to ask him why. What could possibly make a person want life to end?

"You wanted to die?" she repeated in amazement.

"You don't understand. And I don't expect you to. Because you're young. Life is still full of uncharted seas for you. Nineteen is a deceptive time but we need that deception. Now don't look so disturbed," he said, noticing her expression. "I don't feel that way anymore. Wanting death, that is."

They were both silent. Julia was keenly aware of his hand holding hers, warm inside the fleece pocket. In her mind, she heard his voice saying "you are beautiful" over and over.

"I have something to tell you," Aiden said moments later. "But I actually had to take a drink before so I could begin."

So that's what I smelled, Julia thought.

He cleared his throat several times then pushed the remainder of his cigarette down into the grass. Julia felt a slight breeze ripple through her hair and cool her hot face. One thing she would always remember from that evening was that a robin had landed by her feet, cocking its small head so it looked up at her.

Why is a bird out this late at night? she thought. *I wonder what's wrong with it. Is it ill?*

Aiden looked down at the bird.

"New Jersey has so many of those," he said. "Robins, I mean. Nebraska has the meadowlark."

"The meadowlark?"

"Yes," he said, closing his eyes. "Such a long time ago. My mother once nursed a baby meadowlark to health. It had fallen from its nest. After that, it followed her around for months. I was told she had such a gentle way with animals, but she especially loved birds. My grandmother used to call her Meadowlark."

"Your mother sounded wonderful."

"Yes, she was."

Aiden sighed.

"I don't recall a lot about her but I do remember bits and pieces. Lots of things I heard secondhand from my grandmother."

He looked at Julia with tenderness, his voice lowering.

"You are a sweet person," he said. "I wanted to tell you something but I find it hard to begin."

It suddenly occurred to Julia that Aiden had not only taken a drink but was in fact quite drunk. His sentences were slurring. He usually spoke in a clipped tone that sounded British.

"I don't like it when people drink," she said, frowning. "Why do you do it?"

"I don't drink very much, Miss --- Miss ---"

He let go of her hand, looking away from her as he spoke.

"I am a coward. Too frightened to tell you how I feel about you, to tell you how much your friendship has meant to me these past weeks. Though I have appreciated and studied the great poets, I myself am no poet. But my feelings for you have sharpened and I feel I must tell you. I awake thinking of you, I go to sleep thinking of you, and most of the day I feel I am thinking of you far too often. Alas, my soul is in distress. What can this be? Certainly it is not lustful passion. It feels deeper than mere affection. It must be….."

"Hush!" Julia said, embarrassed for him. "You are drunk. Stop saying that."

She was frightened and delighted at the same time. His words stunned her. She felt as if she had just been dunked into ice water. What did he mean? Why was he telling her this? She was not yet nineteen years old. She certainly did not want to hear this. Or did she? Wasn't this an answer to what she had dreamed?

Then, all of a sudden, Julia wanted to run. She did not want to be sitting beside Aiden Hunter. She wished he would disappear, at the same time hoping he would never leave. She wanted to be alone so she could analyze his words. Yet she wanted him to say more.

She leaped to her feet, startling him.

"What?" Aiden said. "Where are you going?"

He tried to stand. Wobbling, he reached for her arm to steady himself.

"Please," Julia said. "Please don't say anymore. You don't know what you're saying."

"But I do. I may be a bit tipsy but I know what I am saying."

He reached for her and pulled her to him so that her head lay against his shoulder. His arms went around her back, holding her against him.

"I am so lonely," he whispered. "So lonely."

"I'm sorry," Julia said. "I'm really sorry."

They stood there for several moments, not moving. Julia had an out-of-body experience, not believing her teacher was embracing her. Yet it did not feel at all sensual.

"Please," he said, "please don't go just yet. I want you to stay."

"I'm not going anywhere. But this whole thing is scaring me. I have to tell you. You are scaring me."

They stood in the darkness for what felt like eternity though only minutes had passed.

"All right," he said.

He lightened his grip on her and put his hands on both sides of her face. Julia looked into his very dark brown eyes. Never before had he been this close to her. It was nothing like the way she had imagined it.

"You are the purest thing I've ever found," he told her. "Pure goodness. Innocence. You are without guile. I've never known anyone like you. I want you to know you make me happy."

I'm not good, Julia thought. *Why does he think that I am?*

Aiden dropped his hands to his side.

"My apologies," he said. "I forgot myself. I didn't mean to offend you. Or frighten you."

I'm not offended. But I am frightened.

The romantic yearnings Julia had felt for him were gone. It was so very confusing.

"Do you care for me as well?" he said. "I hope that you do."

"Yes," she said, more as a pronouncement to herself. As if saying it aloud would make it more real.

* * *

In her dreams that night, Julia was being chased. Though she ran fast, her pursuer was faster. Out of breath, exhausted, she realized she could go no further. A fence blocked her path. She covered her eyes, afraid to see what lie ahead. But her pursuer grabbed her hands, forcing them off her face. Surprised, she stood before a white picket fence surrounding a Cape Cod house with red shutters and flower boxes in the windows. She stared for a long time. It was beautiful. It was perfect in every way.

"Why did you run?" the pursuer asked her. "Isn't this what you always wanted?"

She tried to answer but the words would not come out.

Instead, she thought *yes, this is just the kind of house I always dreamed of, the kind of house I'd have when one day I got married.*

She opened the gate and walked up the cobblestone path to the front door.

I'm safe, she thought, *and I'm finally home.*

She turned to thank the person who had chased her.

I'm so glad you made me open my eyes, she was about to say.

But he had disappeared.

* * *

Ruth Jahns arrived home a little past eleven that night. Tips from her waitressing job jingled in her pocket as she took off her jacket. She checked on her two young sons who were in a sound sleep. Then she made her way up the stairs to her daughter's attic bedroom. As usual, the room was tidy, the books in an orderly pile the desk, the birdcage with its five parakeets covered for the night. She walked over to the dresser to see if the movie projector had been turned on. It had not.

Julia was asleep, covered with a pink flowered coverlet. Ruth bent over to kiss her daughter's forehead. She noticed the peaceful look on Julia's face and smiled. Ruth Jahns felt sudden pity for her friend, Clara Murden, who had agonized to her over the phone about Jenny.

"No wild ways for my daughter," she whispered to herself as she made her way down the stairs, looking forward to a hot cup of tea. "I have the most perfect child."

And though she knew it was not the least bit Christian of her, she felt smug.

CHAPTER SIX

The boy sat on his father's tractor, a baby bird he had rescued nestled on his lap. The day was darkening but he liked to sit by himself looking out at the cornfield. The vastness of land was so beautiful. It was here he could retreat from farm chores, his father's critical remarks and Guenther's teasing. He wished with all his heart that his grandmother would return. After his mother died, Grandma stayed with them a long time. But she had to go home and now her visits were only twice a year. Grandma told him stories of his mother and how she was an angel in heaven with beautiful wings. "She was wonderful," Grandma said, "With a pure and sensitive heart." Life, she told him, can sometimes become unbearable. Then Grandma would cry, remembering her young daughter. The boy would pat her arm but that made her cry harder. Other times Grandma didn't weep at all, but instead got mad at the boy's father when she heard him scream at his older son. Why did he so blatantly favor Guenther? She'd tell her grandson to forgive his daddy, that he wasn't the same man after Mama died. The boy was too angry to forgive his father but he held it in. He held everything in. He was so quiet that his father thought him "addled".

Aiden was not at school the following day. Sandee Dee found Julia by the cafeteria and handed her an envelope.

"Dr. Hunter is at an all-day meeting off campus but phoned and said to find you and give this message to you right away."

Sandee looked at Julia with a raised eyebrow.

"It looks important. Not like Professor Hunter to act so excitable on the telephone and have me run all over the place looking for a student."

"I, I think he needs me to find a file we lost the other day," Julia fibbed. "I know he said it was very important."

"Yes, well, whatever floats your boat. I must get back to my desk. Enjoy your day."

Julia waited till Sandee left before reading the note.

"I have a seminar tomorrow at Lee University in Billerton off Route 99," the message read. "It might last till early evening. Could you possibly meet me there at noon on Saturday to assist? If so, arrive in front at the Humanities Building." It was signed "A. Hunter".

She folded the paper and stuck it in her purse, hands shaking. Her emotions were still in a jumble over the previous night's events. Aiden Hunter loved her and needed her! She still could not believe what had happened between them. And though he hadn't said "I love you" outright, he had certainly insinuated it. The concept made her feel comforted but she was not ecstatic. Why? She did not know.

Tomorrow was Saturday. He wanted her to meet him on a weekend at a campus miles away. It was strange. But she knew she would go.

Is this love? she thought, as she went through the rest of the day. *I want to see him but I'm not daydreaming about it.*

It was so troubling. But wasn't that part of love? Jenny had always told her that love would have its ups and downs. Then again, what did Jenny know? Julia couldn't ask her mother. She had never heard her mother or aunt talk about being in love. And there was no way she could ever tell her mother about Aiden Hunter. She would only worry and imagine the worst. Best to keep quiet. Let things happen naturally.

Saturday came. Mrs. Jahns was busy doing laundry and caring for her two young sons. She thought nothing of it when her daughter told her goodbye and said she'd be gone for the day. In the past Julia always went out on Saturdays, either to walk downtown to the library or meet the twins. On this day, Julia told her mother she'd call her later but wouldn't be late.

"Just to remind you, Jenny phoned last night but I told her you were sleeping," her mother said. "She said it was important you get back to her today."

As she drove down the highway toward Billerton, Julia dismissed the thought of Jenny Murden and her problem. No doubt the call was to let Julia know she was either pregnant or relieved that she was not. In the past, Julia always returned calls from her friends, scared they would get mad at her. But something felt different. Now that she knew Aiden cared for her, she was no longer scared. At that moment, she decided it was over. Never again would she call or talk to Laine or Jenny Murden. In fact, she did not want to see either one of them ever again.

* * *

Lee University consisted of five brick buildings on a tree-lined street abutting Route 99, two blocks from the city of Tilletson. Julia found the humanities building and pulled into the parking lot. Getting out of her car, she saw a familiar figure walking towards her. Aiden's black hair ruffled up in the breeze, his eyes squinting in the sunlight.

"You got my note, I see," he said. "I hope you'll excuse the lie but the staff at Raleigh are such gossips."

"You aren't having an all-day seminar?"

"Why, no. I wanted to see you. I hope you don't mind."

"No, I don't mind," Julia said. "I did think it was weird you wanting me to work on a weekend."

"That woman who always wears those garish animal print outfits answered the phone. I had her take down the message to give you. I had the feeling she thought I was a predator."

"Sandee Dee? She's unusual, isn't she? I don't think you're one of her favorites."

"Dee? Why she's like a cliché. No matter. I'm glad you are here."

Aiden walked her over to his car. The inside was as messy as his office. He shoved papers off the front seat so she could sit down.

"I was nervous, I must confess, that you wouldn't show up," he said as he started the motor. He breathed a loud, exaggerated sigh then smiled when it jumped to life.

"Aha! It has resurrected!"

Julia laughed. She knew what it was like to drive an old car.

"As I was saying," Aiden continued, maneuvering out of the parking lot. "I was certain you wouldn't show up today. After our conversation. I was afraid I had scared you off. I was a bit intense. Forgive me for that. I usually don't make such a display."

"That's okay," Julia said. "I didn't mind."

A silence ensued.

"I don't know what it is," Aiden said. "But I've felt this pull toward you ever since I first saw you in class. It was just a slight pull, I tried to ignore it. I knew you had left the chocolate on my desk. Varnerum saw you and told me. I was intrigued. Then I thought well, maybe she feels a pull, too. Towards me. I told myself it couldn't be true. You were just so young. How could you possibly entertain the thought of me?"

"You're forty-five?"

"I'll be forty-five on July thirtieth."

"I'll be nineteen on August thirteenth."

The age discrepancy, when spoken, was enough to render them both mute.

"I felt this pull toward you as well," Julia said. "The first time I looked at you teaching a class. I don't even know if you saw me though you had looked up. That's when I decided to switch my class."

He reached for her hand.

"You see, we are of like mind. Now, where shall we drive?" he said. "To a park? There's one not far from my apartment. It is such a beautiful day."

"Yes, it is."

"I normally don't like to walk, I find it boring, but it seems the thing to do on such a day. Did you have lunch?"

"No," Julia said, not wanting to admit she had been too nervous to eat at all.

"Then we shall stop for food as well."

The day went by quickly. Julia forgot about her friends, her mother, her schoolwork and her faith. Being with an older man who cared about everything and anything she said was thrilling. She did not want the feeling to end. And Aiden Hunter did not touch her except to hold her hand.

* * *

"So tell me about your life," Aiden said as they sat down to lunch. "What is it like growing up in this fast moving New Jersey?"

"I don't know," Julia said. "I'm really not the typical New Jersey person."

"Oh?"

"I mean, I grew up in this state, my ancestors go back two hundred years or more and as far as I know, they all lived in New Jersey. But I'm not one to give you any good answers. In fact, I was always a weird teenager."

"So was I. We have that in common. And how would you define weird?"

"I knew I was different when I was thirteen. Before that I probably didn't notice it."

"What happened?"

"I just fell into these --- I don't know, these -- periods of craziness. My aunt called this first one an obsession. I was outside that morning, playing records in the back yard with my friends. We used to put my record player out on the porch and dance. I came inside for a drink and walked by the television set. There was this British man on a show. I stopped to look at him. He was older, in his thirties. From that second on, I was obsessed with him. I had to watch his program every day. And since I was drinking green Gatorade, from then on I associated green Gatorade with him. I had to keep drinking it."

"That's not so bad -- is it?"

"Oh it's bad. It got so bad that I'd get hysterical if I wasn't home to watch the show. My mother bought me an old, used T.V. set for my room. This craziness lasted eighteen months. My mother never spent extra money on anything, but she got me that T.V. set.

"Not so awful, eighteen months."

"When you're thirteen, eighteen months is a long time."

There was a pause. When Aiden smiled, she mistook his affection for dismissal.

He doesn't understand.

"I didn't like school at thirteen," he said. "But for different reasons. I was bright and it bored me. Good grades came effortlessly. I loathed the social part of it all."

"So did I. But I was just an average student."

"So you too disliked the non-academic side?"

"Yes. You don't fit in when you carry on about a man on television who's much older than you and you don't even know him. I started to hate my life in eighth grade. No normal thirteen year old girl acted like I did."

Aiden took her hand.

"I am beginning to believe there is no such thing as normal," he said.

"Oh, you're so wrong!"

"I have lived a lot longer than you. Human beings are complicated. Our brains, our feelings are complicated. Sometimes we ---"

He paused.

"I'm sure you weren't like me at thirteen," she said, wondering what he was thinking.

"Hmmmmmm?"

"I mean, my friends liked the boys in our school, our classmates. At the lunch table, everyone talked about the boy they liked, or the boy who liked them. But I wanted to talk about this old British T.V. star, a person who didn't even know me. I knew I could never talk about it with my friends. I had to keep everything to myself. They thought I was strange to begin with. Then the following year, in ninth grade, I was obsessed with another older man. I made the mistake of telling the twins. They mocked me that entire year."

Julia sighed.

"That was years ago. I'm now an adult and they still regard me as an oddity."

"So they think you're bizarre?"

"Yes!"

She pressed her hands against her temples as if trying to wipe out the memories.

"It was just horrible. You have no idea what I went through. To not like boys at all, to only like older men, when you're only in junior high."

Boys, he thought. *She did not like boys.*

"I was a freak. A total freak."

She paused.

"And that British celebrity. He wasn't even in my life. I never met him. Just a face on T.V. with that English accent."

"Probably better than real life," Aiden said. "Safer."

"But crazy." Julia dropped her eyes. "No one gets that way over someone they've never even met."

"You were sad," Aiden said. "But you knew what you were sad about."

"What?" Julia responded. "Of course I knew. Doesn't everyone know what they're sad about?"

Aiden stood up. He took a cigarette out of his back pocket and fumbled for his lighter.

"I wish you wouldn't smoke. It's not good for you." Julia wrinkled her nose. "I never even tried it."

"Now that's a good thing."

He blew a puff of smoke into the air.

"See, you are full of contradictions," he said. "You don't care what people think, so you claim, and yet you do care. Why fret if your friends thought you odd for liking a man you didn't know? Wouldn't that wall between you and them make you reconsider them as friends?"

She shrugged.

"There was nobody else. I felt like I didn't fit in but at least I wasn't by myself. To be totally alone would be worse."

"Worse than being with people who torment you? Hmmmm? I think solitude would be far preferable."

"Maybe for you. I mean, you live alone and have for a long time. I've only lived with my family. I have never been alone. The thought of that is so scary."

"You can be alone in a crowd," Aiden replied. "You can feel alone with millions of people milling about you. Alone when no one understands you. No one knows how you truly feel, how you truly need....."

His voice drifted off.

"You mean what you truly need?"

Aiden shook his head.

"Some people always look happy," Julia said. "I guess I just am not one of them."

"You are more sensitive. As I was. People like us over-think things and over-analyze. Most people muddle through life just worrying about the next item they need to buy at the store. Or with what to impress their neighbors. The simpletons of life."

Julia looked at him, wondering when he would put the cigarette down and hold her hand.

"We are not the simpletons," he said "So we suffer."

Yes, Julia thought. *I have suffered a lot.* How wise he was!

"My holy roller aunt had a verse that explains a lot of this," Aiden said. "It went something like, with much wisdom comes much sorrow.....the more knowledge, the more grief. Either from the Psalms or Ecclesiastes. I was never one for memorizing scripture. But it's quite true. There are times the not-so-good book does make sense."

"Please don't make fun of God's word."

She said a quick prayer that God would excuse him.

"Don't do that," she repeated. "God's word is holy. Don't mock the scriptures."

Aiden did not appear to hear her.

"Actually that was not an accurate term for my aunt. She was more of a Bible thumper than a holy roller. I couldn't picture Aunt Stella rolling on the floor for anyone. Even God."

"Please don't blaspheme God," she said again. "You don't want to commit the unforgiveable sin!"

He smiled at her panic-stricken face.

"All right," he said. "I hold out hope for a God that is merciful, one who will forgive my many transgressions."

As he walked her back to her car later that day, she was lost in thought.

I like him so much! I wonder if he still likes me? I hope he didn't find me boring.

"I had an enjoyable time, Miss Jahns," he said with a British accent as he opened the door for her. "Farewell and drive safely home."

He took her hand and raised it to his lips.

"I shall only kiss thy hand in parting lest thou thinkest me not a gentleman."

Julia smiled.

"I bet you don't have a drop of English blood in you," she said.

"You're right. I'm mostly Czech."

* * *

The phone rang that Saturday. It reverberated into the empty apartment. No one answered. No one was there to hear it. How unusual, the caller thought.

It rang again several hours later.

The caller put the receiver back into its cradle slowly. He paced the floor of his room for several minutes, wringing his hands.

But the light was on! I saw that the light was on!

Picking up his suede jacket, he plucked away blond strands that had stuck to the material. Annoying how he was suddenly losing his hair. He was too young to be going bald, too young to have his looks fade. Time marches on, it waits for no one. One cannot possibly afford to lose one's attractiveness, not with the competition out there, not with the horror of someday being replaced. The grim mantra of time passing repeated itself in his brain. He punched his fist into the wall by the front door. Then he went out.

* * *

Guenther Hunter stood at the door to his brother's apartment about to ring the doorbell for the fifth time. He was growing impatient. Aiden had said to meet him at four o'clock and it was four twenty. No one was answering the door. And it looked like no one was at home.

The toot of a horn startled him and he turned. His brother, pulling up in front of the building, waved at him. Guenther shook his head.

"Late," he said under his breath. "Always late."

"I should have given you my spare key," Aiden said as he made his way up the steps to where his brother stood. "That way you can pop in anytime you're in town without having to wait."

"At least you're here," Guenther sighed. "I thought you had forgotten."

"No, I hadn't. I see you remain the ever prompt visitor."

The two men went inside. Guenther, tidy and organized, shook his head again, this time at the sight of the apartment.

"You need a housekeeper."

"Clear off some of the debris and sit down," Aiden said, removing his jacket and tossing it on a chair. "Would you like some tea? We have plenty of time before the train leaves."

"Yes, with a lemon slice. You seem out of breath. Were you out all day?"

"Most of the day, yes."

"Oh. I hope I didn't interrupt anything. I must say, it's very nice weather you're having out east. We always hear such negative things about New Jersey. Not that Nebraska's weather is all that much better."

"Springtime can fluctuate. It's full of surprises. Did you say just lemon?"

Guenther followed his brother into the galley kitchen.

"You seem chipper today," Guenther remarked, noticing his brother's cheerfulness. "I guess good weather does affect one's mood."

"Indeed it does."

Aiden filled a kettle and put it on the stove.

"I also spent the day with a delightful person. It's amazing how being with someone you truly like can change one's mood. I awoke feeling sour but now I feel very refreshed."

"Oh?" Guenther's surprise was not lost on his brother.

"Don't look so shocked. I know you consider me the ultimate hermit but every now and then I do come to life."

"By the way," Guenther said. "I found an envelope sticking under your welcome mat. I didn't want to disturb it, didn't want you to think I'm nosy, so it's still there."

"I'll retrieve it later," Aiden said, reaching for the teabags. "It's probably from the landlord. He mentioned wanting to send in a plumber. Have had a nasty leak under the sink for weeks now."

"That's the convenient plus about renting," Guenther said. "Every time something in my house breaks, it's another expense. I am not the least bit handy."

"We do have that in common," Aiden replied. "I can barely change a light bulb."

"Getting back to your outing," Guenther said, watching Aiden busy himself preparing their beverage, "who, if I may ask, was this charming person you spent time with?"

Aiden opened the refrigerator door and took out a lemon. He put it on the counter and began slicing it.

"I enjoy seeing your antenna go up, Guenther. You're just dying to hear something sordid. I so hate to disappoint you. I spent the day with someone who has both youthful enthusiasm and a kind heart. The former, not so much the latter, has rubbed off on me. Sometimes I think it's good to be with the young as I spend far too many hours with grumpy middle-aged professors."

"That's why having children is a blessing," Guenther said. "They grow up to be the youth you can hang around with."

Aiden put two cups on the table and squeezed a lemon slice into his brother's tea. Guenther took a sip, the steam fogging up his eyeglasses.

"Piping hot, just the way I like it," he said.

"As I have no children, I was not afforded the blessing you enjoy, Guenther. But I spent the day with a student, a wonderful young lady. I believe you remember her from the day you were at the college."

"Young lady?" the words slipped out before Guenther could stop them.

"Don't act so shocked. It doesn't become you. You remember my student, Miss Jahns?"

"Yes, I do," Guenther said. "When you said young, I figured thirty years old. She is --- why, she is not more than a child."

"She's an adult," Aiden said, scowling. "Since when is a college student not an adult?"

"Barely," Guenther muttered. "But no matter. I'm assuming the relationship is platonic?"

"You don't mince words do you?"

"I'm sorry, but you are a male and she is a female. It's what comes to mind when you think of a relationship."

"You should have a handyman come in and fix that filter on your mouth. It doesn't seem to be working."

"Now, Aiden," Guenther said, "You don't have to start lashing out at me. I certainly did not mean to offend you. But let's face it, I've met Miss Jahns and she is quite young. Maybe legally an adult but emotionally she seemed very….."

"Very what?"

"Immature. Not all nineteen year old women are women."

"Nevertheless, she is my student, my work-study assistant, but she is also my friend. She is more than just a person of nineteen years. And she is not like all my other students with their varying degrees of dizziness. She is quite serious, someone who looks beyond the surface of things. She is also quite spiritual, something I'm sure you would be pleased with."

"She is a Christian?"

Guenther rarely brought up his faith with his brother, knowing Aiden to be a hostile agnostic.

"Yes, she is. And perhaps that is also what makes her more mature than, ahem, many of the thirty year olds you cite."

"I didn't know her Christian faith would be an asset in your view. And she is fond of you as well? That is welcome news. It's good to have found a friend. I am supposing she has a boyfriend? Would that boyfriend object to your friendship?"

"I never asked her about her boyfriends," Aiden said. "It's none of my concern."

"I think it should be —-"

"I've suddenly lost interest in this subject. Are you here to continue to pry into my life or are you here to visit and go into New York with me?"

"Why are you so defensive, Aiden? You brought the subject up. I'm merely asking you why a college girl would want to befriend a much older man. It appears unusual. And if she does indeed have a boyfriend, which most college girls these days do have, it just seems ---"

"I want to end the subject," Aiden said, annoyed. "I'm sorry I brought it up."

Good mood evaporating, he was suddenly sick of talking to his brother. Leave it to Guenther to ruin another conversation.

"This will cease to be tonight's topic of discussion."

Guenther sighed and put up his hands in surrender.

"Subject now changed. I can see you are still the very private man."

"I am private because of how things get twisted as you have twisted my words."

Aiden could feel anger rising up in him. For a moment, he wanted to strike Guenther and be rid of his condescending airs.

Still at it, aren't you Guenther? I'm the loser and you're the anointed one!

"I didn't mean to twist anything. I'm truly sorry, Aiden. We are going to dinner tonight and I am just glad to spend the time with you. I'm also happy you have made a new friend. Let us leave it at that."

He watched his brother rinse out the kettle and suddenly felt sad. He did not like to pity anyone but Aiden seemed to him to be a pathetic creature.

No doubt the young girl's interest was merely a figment of a lonely man's imagination.

"So getting on to other things, how do you like working at a junior college?" Guenther said, feigning cheeriness. "I can't believe how long you've stayed at your position. Not to be insulting, but we all had you pegged for greater things. You were one of the brightest students in your graduating class. I always pictured you one day teaching at an Ivy League university. Or even discovering a cure for cancer."

"Destiny thought differently and here I am. As of today, I am content."

"That is good to hear. I hope you stay with such a mindset.

Guenther picked up his cup of tea and raised it into the air.

"Here's a toast then to my brother's newfound sense of peace," he said. "May it always be so."

* * *

Jenny Murden drove to Julia's house, furious she was being ignored. It was three o'clock in the afternoon and she did not see Julia's car in the driveway. She was sure Mrs. Jahns was home because her old green Impala was parked in front of the house.

Jenny knocked on the door. After a few moments, Julia's mother opened it, drying her hands on a dish towel.

"Hello, Jenny. Come on inside. I haven't seen you in quite a while."

"I didn't mean to come over without calling but I wanted to see if I could talk to Julia before I went out."

"Why, Julia left around eleven thirty this morning," Mrs. Jahns said in surprise. "I just assumed she was with Laine."

"No, Laine's home in bed with a cold. Where do you think she went?"

"I have no idea. Julia's been extra quiet lately. Maybe she just needed some time alone. This place is so small and her brothers don't give her a moment's peace."

Jenny's face was flushed and her eyes blinked continuously.

"Is anything wrong, Jenny? Do you want to come in?"

"No. I guess, well, I'll just call her later. Or have her call me. It's really nothing. I was just hoping to catch her."

"I did tell her before she left that you had called. I'm sure she'll get back to you."

Jenny scowled.

"She's been avoiding me and my sister. But I guess if that's the way she wants it to be, then that's okay."

"I'm sure you girls will straighten things out," Mrs. Jahns said. The frown remained on Jenny's face but she ignored it.

"I will remind her that you were here, dear. And say hello to your mother for me."

* * *

Julia spent the next several Saturdays meeting Aiden Hunter in the Lee University parking lot. They would spend their days together walking through the park, eating lunch, visiting museums or picking out books in the library. A few times he took her to the local theatre. Because of their continuing friendship, Julia had decided in late March to drop Aiden's class. She did not want to cause him any problems in case someone noticed them together. Unfortunately, she had to submit her "release from class" form to Sandee Dee. Sandee, usually chatty and vivacious, said little and eyed Julia with disapproval.

"English Lit not to your liking?" she said as she stamped the form and filed it. "I personally have no interest in dead limey writers."

"Just don't have the time," Julia lied. "It was only for extra credits anyway."

"Really? Well I do see you need one speech class. Would you like to sign up for next semester?"

"No, I don't know what I'll be doing next fall," Julia said. "But I'll keep it in mind."

Julia did not want to spend much time talking to Sandee, whom she now pegged as a dangerous gossip. The old woman had befriended Laine and Jenny for Julia often saw them talking by Sandee's desk. Sandee no longer waved or joked with Julia when she bumped into her in the hall. Who knew what vicious rumors the twins and Sandee were spreading? It was best to avoid all of them.

Aiden agreed with her.

"It won't hurt for you to continue the work-study program with me," he had told her one Saturday. "But I suspect several people have noticed our friendship and it's wise you not remain my student."

Julia had not returned any of Jenny's calls. Any free time Julia had on campus she spent in the library, avoiding the student lounge where her friends hung out. March turned into April. In due time, Aiden's once empty vase was filled with dandelions.

By mid-April, Jenny and Laine had ceased their phone calls to Julia's house. The times the two sisters bumped into her at school, they turned their heads. It was such a relief to have them angry with her. Through a classmate's chatter, Julia learned that Jenny had not gotten pregnant after all though Craig McCrory had dumped her. Word spreads fast in a junior college. Each week Jenny walked through the halls clinging to the arm of a different boyfriend.

Spring is a season of love, Julia thought one Saturday as she drove to meet Aiden. *And I feel like I do love Aiden Hunter!*

It was ironic because for some reason, she could not call him by his first name. She tried to once but felt the word stick on her tongue. And so she avoided calling him anything. She noticed he did not refer to her as "Julia" but "Miss Jahns". It was actually kind of nice. She felt Aiden to be the perfect gentleman, always respectful with impeccable manners. He was both charming and interesting. Being naïve, she did not see anything unusual in his subdued behavior. That he never attempted to kiss her or grope her in any way did not feel the least bit out of the ordinary.

Julia never questioned what Aiden did with the rest of his weekend. They had gotten to a point where she sensed some things were better left unsaid. He never spoke of the previous ten years of his life before he had come to Crane Ridge to teach. She felt it would be nosy to pry so she did not question him. Aiden also did not ask her about what she did when she was not with him. Just being in her company gave him pleasure and he looked forward to the days spent with her.

Sometimes when he looked at Julia, a torrent of emotion welled up inside. He did not try to analyze his feelings but just relished them. He had no desire to take her into his arms or kiss her. His affection rose to a higher plane than mere love because to him, romantic love harbored lust. Julia's caring friendship, respect for his privacy and inexperience all combined to make her irresistible. She asked nothing of him except his company. He had never before felt anyone had ever truly belonged to him. Until now.

* * *

School came to an end the first week in May. Julia lined up a summer job as a typist in a small office in Crane Ridge. Aiden walked to the campus library with her that last day and she told him of her plans.

"I shall miss you working for me during the week," he said. "But we will still be together on Saturdays I am assuming?"

"Of course. That isn't changing."

"So who is this new employer you'll be working for?"

"Some lawyer named Douglas Shaw. He used to work with my cousin Ned, that's how I got the job. I know nothing about law but he's going to teach me. It's just a summer position anyway."

She was flattered that Aiden looked depressed.

"You won't find him more interesting than you do me?"

"Don't be silly. He's a thirty-year-old married man with kids. I'm just working there because I need the money. Raleigh won't let us work here during the summer."

"I feel out of sorts about it. And I shall miss your presence. I've gotten used to seeing you in my office. Things will feel lonely."

"Only a few months and I'll be back."

"Time goes by so slowly," Aiden sighed. "And when you want it to go quickly, it does not."

"Just think of me when you miss me and know I'll be back soon."

I feel like you're my very best friend and I love you!

The words echoed through her thoughts but she could not say them out loud. Why?

"I care for you so much," Aiden said, taking her hand. "I hope that you will always care for me."

"Yes," she said. "Always."

* * *

The college halls were empty. Very few professors were around, most of them gone for the summer break. It was an unusually cool day for May. On the west wing of the Humanities building, a light was on in a corner office.

"Hello there."

Aiden Hunter looked up from his book.

"The light was on. On such a sunny day and you have the light on?"

Aiden's heart began fluttering. Was it fear or anticipation?

"Hold on," he said. He stood and closed his book.

The figure in the doorway did not move.

"Did you get my note? I left it at your apartment. Under the mat."

"Give me a moment," Aiden said. "What note?"

"Never mind. I've missed you. It's been a long time."

"Please don't say anything. You never know if someone is still here."

"Your light was on."

"Yes. Yes, I know."

Aiden grabbed his briefcase and followed the figure as he made his way down the hall, out the side door to the back parking lot.

"I've missed you."

"Not here," Aiden repeated. "Please."

"Calm down. I'll follow your car. I won't say anything else."

Aiden nodded. He got into his blue Fiat, turned on the motor and watched as the young man walked away.

* * *

Guenther Hunter telephoned his brother in the middle of May.

"I'm flying east again soon, Aiden," he said. "My son is looking at colleges. I am leaving him with some friends in New York who are taking him around, then returning home. Will you be free one day for a visit?"

"I suppose so. What day would that be?"

"A Sunday. I believe that's May twenty-fifth."

"All right."

"I'll rent a car and drive over. How have things been?"

"Right now all is well."

"Right now?"

"Yes, for now all is fine. Who knows the future?"

"Well that's true enough. But who wants to know the future? I certainly do not. What's the matter, Aiden, you sound blue."

"Do I? School has ended for the semester. It's odd but this time of year is always a letdown for me."

"I just hope you have cut back on your drinking. I'm not saying that to be self-righteous. When you get depressed you tend to overdo the booz. I'm concerned for your health."

"My health is just jolly fine."

Guenther, you haven't changed; still the same Dudley Do-Right!

Swallowing his annoyance, he changed the subject.

"So are you still a married man? Has the divorce been finalized?"

"Virginia's filed. Not yet final. I should have seen this whole thing coming. I've been so busy over the years building up my practice. Now that I have three doctors working for me and can take time off, I lost a wife. She fell in love with someone else."

"Yes, you told me. You realize everyone is divorcing these days."

"I know. It's getting to be quite the trend."

Guenther sighed.

"I can't regret any of it, though. I have five beautiful children from my marriage. Where would I be without them? My Shelley might be getting engaged soon, by the way. I can't believe how fast she's grown up."

There was a pause.

"Speaking of nineteen year old young ladies," Guenther said. "How is your friend doing?"

"She is doing quite well," Aiden replied. "I was waiting for you to bring the subject up again."

"Don't be snide, Aiden, it was just a question."

"Yes, well, whatever you say. Miss Jahns isn't working for me as the school year is over. But we still have been spending a lot of time together."

"Are you now?"

"As I told you, we are very good friends. I like her a great deal. In fact ---"

Aiden hesitated.

"I think about her quite a bit. I see her every Saturday. I'm find it troubling that I am caring so much. Now that she's gotten another job, I feel she might slip away from me."

Guenther's eyes widened, much to Aiden's annoyance

"Am I hearing you correctly? You are now carrying on with that young girl? A student, no less!"

Guenther's shock was evident in his voice but Aiden also heard contempt. He tried hard to keep his response civil.

"Carrying on? I resent your implication, Guenther. Have you ever had a relationship with someone that was based on something other than carnality?"

"Don't get huffy with me, Aiden. You know exactly why this is a shock. And this girl is a student in a college where you are employed. You are treading in dangerous waters."

Aiden did not hear him.

"I have never met anyone like this person. I can't even put it into words. I am happy in her presence. She is without guile, without any maliciousness."

"I take it then you love her as anyone would love a dear friend."

"It's hard to explain. She has an old soul. I feel like she's always known me. To be honest, the whole thing frightens me. I am caring too much."

"That is the chance you take when you love," Guenther replied. "She is just so very young. People her age don't stay with things long."

"What do you mean?"

"If you love her, you might get hurt. Young ones tend to be fickle, they don't really know what they want at such an age."

"I know she cares for me."

"I am sure she does. Right now. Does she have parents? A father? Maybe she is looking to you as a father figure."

"I don't think that has anything to do with it."

Aiden's candidness made Guenther suspect he had been drinking.

"Do you feel you want more from her?" Guenther tried to be diplomatic. He did not want to infuriate his brother and stop their communication.

"More of what?"

"I don't know how to ask this without getting you angry. Do you want to be intimate with her? Are you at all physically attracted to her?"

"That is a very intrusive question."

"I ask because --- I'm sure you know why I ask."

"The answer is no. That is not even in my thoughts."

"Then it is friendship. A deep friendship."

"It's more than that."

Aiden found it hard to put into words what he himself could not understand.

"Whatever it is, Aiden, I pray you do not get hurt. Because Lord knows, you've been hurt enough."

* * *

Sandee Dee left Raleigh College that May, glad it was summer break. Though she had a job lined up in the nearby town of Quinton as a bus driver, she looked forward to having more time to herself. Working at Raleigh, she put in long hours. Now that summer had arrived, she wouldn't have to report back to work at the college till mid-July. September would come too soon and with it, longer hours. She was getting tired of her job. She envied her female coworkers who had husbands and sought employment out of boredom.

"It's 1975 and I'm supposed to be liberated," she thought as she cleaned out her desk. "Marone! If this is liberation then I have a bone to pick with Susan B. Anthony!"

She eyed two female professors who were laughing together in the hallway.

"It must be nice to get a big paycheck and have no bills to worry about," she muttered to herself as walked to her car. Sometimes she regretted never having remarried. She sure had plenty of offers in her heyday!

"Although at this point in time," she thought, "I don't need no man telling me what to do."

The phone was ringing as she walked into her living room, dropping her pocketbook and lunch bag onto the floor.

"Hold your horses, I'm not as young as I used to be," she said, irritated. Talking to herself had become a habit these days as her kids rarely called, too busy with their own lives.

"Hello," she said into the receiver. Not hearing anyone, she said "Hello, hello?"

"It's me, Auntie," a voice said. "I'm sorry to bother you."

"Oh luv, how are you?" Sandee's mood brightened. "How's my handsome favorite nephew? So glad you called me. I just got in the door. Were you in school last week? I didn't see you. I hope you know on the days you're in to stop by my desk. Today was my last day till July."

"I wasn't in last week. Well, I wasn't in for any classes. I need to talk to you."

"Of course, luv," Sandee said, her voice soothing. "Do you want to come over? I hope nothing's wrong. I'll make us some iced tea and we can chat. You know you can drop in on me anytime."

"I think I will. I'm very upset. I need to ask you a few things."

"Why, luv, of course. Why are you upset? Nothing is wrong is it? You're like a son to me, I hate to hear that you're upset."

"I can be there in an hour."

"Good, I'll be here. Take your time, don't get into any accidents."

"Thanks."

"Okay, Louis luv, see you soon."

Worried, she hung up the phone.

CHAPTER SEVEN

He was fourteen and hated school. Not the lessons themselves because he was very bright and the work was effortless. He hated the forced socialization, the fact that he was always being compared to his brother. Guenther at thirteen was powerfully built, the best player on the softball team, and intelligent as well. He made friends easily. Father always beamed when Guenther and his buddies came home from school, crowding around the kitchen table, noisy, drinking lemonade, and good-naturedly teasing each other. Father would look at his older son, smaller, weak, always hanging back. Like a little shadow, Father called him. Never had his father known anyone so introverted. The boy spent his days in the field, reading. Father did not pat him affectionately on the head or wrestle him to the ground in a bear hug like he did Guenther. Father never touched him at all except to express displeasure. Grandmother had died a year earlier and the boy felt no one cared about him anymore. His sensitive nature began hardening in self-preservation. He couldn't wait for his eighteenth birthday when he could go to college and leave forever. The only thing he would miss was Mr. Schweenhardt. For some reason the boy's heart felt happy every time he was near his teacher. When Mr. Schweenhardt put a fatherly arm around his shoulders, the boy had a mad desire to throw himself in his arms. Then he'd feel ashamed. So ashamed that at times he'd sneak Father's whiskey out of the cupboard and take a swig. When he felt he had numbed his emotions, he'd put the bottle back. If Father ever knew, he would kill him, of that he was certain.

Julia started her first day of work at the law firm with a bad headache. She never got headaches. The day could not have ended fast enough. All she wanted was to go home and lie down with a hot rag on her forehead.

As she was getting ready to leave, the phone rang.

"It's just me, sweetie," Mrs. Jahns said when Julia picked up. "I hate to call you at your new job."

"It's okay, Mom. I was just leaving."

"I'm going to work soon and wanted to let you know you had a phone call. Someone from the college. I didn't want to leave you a note because I thought you might not see it. I wrote down the phone number and left it on your bed. The man sounded nervous."

"It was a man?"

"Yes, I think he said his name was Mr. Gunder. Something like that."

"Mr. Gunder?" Julia was puzzled. Could she have meant to say Guenther?

"I'm not sure, it sounded like Gunder. Anyway, he said to call him, that it was important."

She felt anxious. If it were Guenther Hunter, could something be wrong with Aiden?

"Ned's picking up the boys and taking them to your aunt's," Mrs. Jahns continued. "I'm so glad Aunt Margie quit her job and is able to have them over so often. It finally frees you up. You've been my angel, watching them in your free time all these years."

"I didn't mind."

"That's why you're the best daughter a woman could ask for. Now, before I forget, Clara Murden also called. I didn't like her tone. I guess she's very upset over you not seeing her girls anymore. She said she misses you at church. I told her Clara, they're all grown women now, let them handle their own lives."

Clara Murden should only know what her daughters are like, Julia thought. *Church-going phony baloneys.*

Driving home, she felt on edge. Though she had given Aiden her home number, he had never once called her. She found the note on her bed and dialed the number.

"Thank you for getting back to me so quickly, Julia," a male voice said. "This is Guenther Hunter. I apologize for telling you mother it was Raleigh College calling. I didn't want to interfere in your life. I am not at the college, but I'm calling on behalf of my brother. I am in Aiden's apartment."

"I hope nothing is wrong."

"He fainted in his classroom this morning. He was substituting for a professor who called out, he wasn't even supposed to be there. The school called his apartment and as luck would have it, I was there. What are the chances of that?"

"Is he okay?"

"He's fine now. I told him to go to the doctor to get things checked out but he's very stubborn. He's in the next room, furious that I am calling you."

"That's silly. I told him he could always call me."

"He has too much pride for his own good. He needs to see a doctor. He's being very foolish."

"Let me talk to him."

Guenther called out to his brother and Julia could hear the two of them arguing.

"I'm afraid he is too angry with me to come to the phone."

"Tell him that I said he should go to his doctor."

"He thinks because I myself am a physician that I see disease in every face. Not true. When he fainted he also fell and struck his head. It needs to be checked."

Again, Julia heard the sound of muffled arguing.

"I'm sorry, Julia," Guenther said when he came back to the phone. "I know what the problem is. I'm sorry to have bothered you."

* * *

Sandee spent the next three days sick to her stomach.

She wished she had never let her nephew confide in her. Wished she had never invited him over. Ignorance is truly bliss. Now there was no way she could un-know what she wished she had never heard.

"He's like my son, my sister's only child, and he's twisted," she thought. She felt like crying. But fury overpowered her tears.

"I'm glad Amelia is dead, rest her soul, for she would collapse in grief if she knew what I now know."

Her ponderings went from wanting to kill herself to deep anger. But anger at whom? Her no-good brother-in-law, the drunk Polack who used to beat Louis, or fury directed at someone else? Her brother-in-law had been dead for two years, fatally wounded in a bar fight. She wished he were alive at this moment so she could murder him herself.

"It's his fault," she muttered as she paced the floor soon after Louis had left. "My sister never should have married that rodent. Cut her life short and ruined my nephew's life."

Then she recalled another man, a man who was very much alive. For days the thought of revenge would not leave her mind.

"Whatever is wrong with Louis, that demented man used and abused. Something has got to be done before he hurts more young men. If it takes my last breath, I will see to it that he pays."

* * *

One summer Saturday on a hot and humid morning, Julia decided she and Aiden Hunter should go down the shore. The idea surprised her for she had never been fond of the beach. But there was a longing to see it with him that she could not shake. And so she mentioned it to him.

"So were are going to the famous seashore?" Aiden said when she told him of her plans. "Does this stem from my fainting spell? Do you think the salt air might improve my health?"

"I know you're making fun of me, but I'm serious," Julia replied. "You live in a dirty city in a cramped apartment. It's healthy for you to get some fresh air. Do you like the shore?"

"You mean that vast body of salt water called an ocean? I don't know. I've never been there."

"You've been living in New Jersey for ten years and have never been down the shore?"

"I'm afraid not."

Being a New Jerseyan her entire life, Julia could not imagine a person never having seen the waves, heard the roar of the tide or taken in the delicious air that only the sea could provide. And not have walked the boardwalk? Her earliest memories revolved around the Jersey shore: buying boxes of taffy, holding Aunt Margie's hand as her rubber flip-flops slapped along the weathered planks. She never forgot the smell of cotton candy, fried foods and popcorn; the sound of game hawkers yelling "take a chance, win a prize." The thrill she had felt when her aunt splurged one day, putting a quarter on a number and winning Julia a doll. Her parents never would have gambled away twenty-five cents but Aunt Margie did.

"And I still have that Pebbles Flintstone doll," she told Aiden.

So they went to the Jersey shore and Aiden Hunter saw the Atlantic Ocean for the first time in his life.

"I am not walking in that sand," he said as he watched her remove her sneakers. "But you are right, the view is very nice."

"Smell that air," she said, inhaling deeply. "I love that especially."

"I was never a person who cared to sit and bake on the beach," she said later when they walked down the boardwalk. "I always thought that extremely boring. But to see the seagulls fly by and watch the ocean itself, to me it is beautiful."

"And people swim in that ocean?"

"It's only June so it's cold. By August, if the summer is hot enough, the water warms up."

She picked up a seashell, examining it for cracks.

"I remember seeing a lot more shells when I was a child. There doesn't seem to be as many now. Or maybe my memories are just wishful thinking."

"Childhood memories aren't always accurate."

"That's true."

"And how was your childhood?"

"I felt like I had a very happy childhood till I was around eleven. Then my parents started fighting. My father left soon after that and my mother didn't take us to the ocean much. It was too painful for her. But at least I feel fortunate to have had some good years."

Aiden took her hand.

"When you're a child, time passes so slowly. But now I find I can barely remember myself as a boy."

"What kind of child were you?"

"I don't often think on it."

"You were very little when your mother died. Do you remember her at all?"

"Not really. I do have a memory of being very happy though it didn't last. Most of my childhood was lonely. My father resented being left with two small sons although I know he saw Guenther as a replication of himself. Guenther was strong and athletic, I was not. As we got older, my brother became the proverbial fair-haired son and I the whipping boy. But that is neither here nor there. I don't like to think about it."

Aiden looked up to see a half a dozen seagulls swooping down, then circling, crying out to one another.

"How did your mother die?" Julia asked.

"An accident."

"She wasn't sick?"

"No. We were told – Guenther and I – that she had an accident in the shed. An old shelf full of farm tools had dislodged and fell down on her. My grandmother said she probably didn't know what hit her."

"So she didn't suffer."

"Most likely not."

"I'm sure she's been in heaven all these years watching over you. She's your guardian angel."

Aiden's laugh was scornful.

"She would've served a better purpose by remaining on earth as my mother. I don't believe in an afterlife. But don't let me water down your beliefs. I am sure you find solace in them."

"If I believe it or not, if heaven is real, then it's real."

"And if it's not?"

"I choose to believe it is."

"If I believed in an afterlife, which I do not, I'd prefer the concept of reincarnation. I should like to come back as a bird. That to me would be a reward for my good deeds. If indeed, I have any."

"So coming back as a person would be the punishment?"

"My idea of hell, yes. Humanity is far too painful. People strive for happiness all their lives, chasing dreams. They attain them and are happy for so many years or months, only to have them snatched away by death. Or they never achieve them and spend their days feeling wretched. Either way it's misery. I only hope our conscious existence takes us down that road once. I shudder to think of it any other way."

"I believe there's something better ahead," Julia said. "And that gives me hope. Without hope, what do you have?"

"Despair."

Aiden walked over to a bench, looking out at the ocean.

"I don't mean to continue quibbling with you about your faith," he said after a long pause. "But if you're a thinking person, and I know that you are, this whole thing has to be a pile of rubbish."

"The Christian faith?"

"Ponder it. Let us say you become a believer when you're thirty or forty years old. You now believe in a heaven and a hell and all that. But you realize your parents, and maybe your grandparents, whom you loved, have died long ago. They were not believers. Maybe they were atheists or at the very least, agnostics. How can you then ascribe to a faith that would put your loved ones in a place of eternal torment? For I believe that is what you Christians think hell is."

Aiden's dilemma was hers at one time. She had prayed hard to find an answer and it had come one day out of nowhere.

"I have such a faith in God to realize He knew beforehand who would choose Him and who would not," she said. "But even if they had always mocked religion or shaken their fist at God, at that very last second before they died, they'd cling to Him and go to heaven. I feel God's love for us is that powerful. Nothing can move it."

"So only the truly evil would reject such a gift."

"Yes. Only wicked people would see hell approaching and embrace it."

"Your reasoning is interesting. I admire your convictions."

He looked at her and again something stirred inside his heart. Like the gulls flying skyward and then swooping down around them, he felt his emotions soar with love for her. "That's why they call it falling in love," he had once heard a coworker explain. It was true. It was like falling from a cliff in slow motion.

I love you so, he wanted to tell her. Why couldn't he?

The sun shone on her dark blond hair, her blue eyes bright, squinting at him behind the large glasses. She looked like an angel. He would remember that moment forever. An old love had reawakened inside and transferred itself to her.

Julia noticed his face change and his eyes soften. She looked away, embarrassed. Enjoying their discussion, she was surprised that his sudden look of affection annoyed her.

Sensing her discomfort, the moment of his intense longing for her was gone almost as soon as it had appeared.

"Speaking of hell," Aiden said after a few minutes. "My brother keeps insisting I go back to Nebraska for a visit. I have seen more of him in the past couple of months than I saw for twenty years."

"Are you going to go?"

"If I had gone, it would have been today. I have no desire to ever go back there. I am sure Guenther's sudden surge of brotherly interest has occurred because his wife is gone. And he's getting older. Some people become very nostalgic as they age."

"It's nice that he cares so much. He seems like a very nice person."

Aiden took a cigarette out of his pocket and lit it.

"Guenther and I are two totally different people. He has time to think of me now that he's alone. I'm sure he will soon find another wife, knowing him. Which is a good thing because if we started seeing each other frequently, we would not get along."

Julia was at a loss. She could not picture herself getting older and not having a relationship with her brothers.

"He must love you an awful lot to call me up in a panic over your getting sick that day," she said. "And he's making an effort to visit you."

"He's been nagging me to visit Nebraska and see the family. Rather, *his* family. It's ridiculous. I have no relationship with his children. I left a long time ago."

"It's your home state. It probably has changed since you were last there. It might wind up being a fun thing to do, seeing relatives and such."

"I'd rather have a tooth pulled. Nebraska does not hold many good memories for me."

Julia understood. Sometimes she felt that way about New Jersey.

"Getting off the subject of my brother," Aiden said. "I would like to broach another matter with you. Do you realize that this fall will begin the last year of your studies at Raleigh? Have you thought about what you're going to do after that?"

Aiden sat down on the bench and motioned for her to follow suit.

"I really don't know," Julia replied. "I've heard the twins are both going away to finish up their last two years and get bachelor's degrees. But I don't want to."

"Go away or get a degree?"

"Well, I will have my associate's degree by next year," she said. "But to get a four year degree will mean I'd have to go away to another college. I'd have to live there which I don't want to do. I just don't want to leave home."

"Then you will forfeit a degree you might desire one day."

"Maybe I'll get a job somewhere. Actually, I don't like to think about it. I've been putting the topic out of my mind."

"It's not that far away, it might be best to think on it."

"A year from now seems very far away."

"Yes, I guess it does when you're not yet twenty. To me, a year feels like the twinkling of an eye."

"To me, it feels like an eternity. Maybe next year when I'm turning twenty, I will know what I want to do."

"Whatever you decide, I hope we are together."

She put her hand over his hand.

"Of course we will. Why wouldn't we be?"

"I don't know," he said. "I just know that talking with you always makes me feel better." *And younger, and full of hope*

They were both quiet as they watched the tide come in.

I'm so glad, he thought, *that I am here with you and not with Guenther in Nebraska.*

* * *

Julia arrived home that evening with a sunburned face. Mrs. Jahns was standing at the front door when her car pulled up. It was five o'clock and Julia realized her mother would soon be leaving for work.

"I'll baby-sit Rob and Eddie," Julia said after greeting her mother. "I'm not doing anything tonight."

"How was your trip to the beach?"

"Just fine. It was a hot drive down but it's always cool by the water."

"Did you go with those girls you used to work with at Roote's? What were their names again? Mary Ann and ---"

"Mary Lou Sipaski and Pammy Haus? Why, no. Someone else --- a friend from school. I couldn't believe the lack of crowds. For a hot June day, hardly anyone was there."

Mrs. Jahns shook her head.

"Are you sure you don't want to say anything else?"

Julia stopped emptying her bag. She felt sudden tension in the air.

"What do you want me to tell you?"

"Someone phoned me today and said she worked at the college. She told me as a mother, she was concerned about who my daughter has been keeping company with."

"Someone from *my school* called you?"

"Yes. She said she was a divorced woman who raised three kids and a nephew. Because she knew of my situation, she wanted to let me know that I should start asking some questions about your friends."

"Was this someone named Sandee?"

"Yes."

Julia shook her head. She followed her mother into the kitchen and sat down at the table.

"Mom, please sit with me for a second."

"I have to leave for work soon but this is important. She got me quite upset."

"Look, Mom, Sandee is a busybody. She's also friendly with the twins. She's the person who got us the work-study jobs. The twins like her because she's loud and a gossip. They blow everything out of proportion. I wouldn't put it past Sandee to call you because the twins are angry with me."

"She didn't sound like a busybody. She sounded concerned. I asked her whom I should be worried about and she said to ask *you*. So I'm here asking."

"Sandee's crazy."

"Who was she referring to?"

"No one. I avoid the twins now and they're spreading gossip and lies. All because I won't go out with this guy Louis, a friend of theirs. From now on, if either one of them calls me, tell them I'm not interested. I'm never talking to them again."

"It just seemed strange that an older woman, an employee of a college, would call here unless," Mrs. Jahns paused. "Well, I believe you. I know how Jenny and Laine can be. They've always been jealous of you. And after all, I'm the one who said you should find better friends."

"That's the trouble. I made better friends and they don't like it."

Mrs. Jahns smiled, relieved. She knew she could trust her daughter.

"I'm so glad, dear, I really am. Now I can go to work with peace of mind."

Julia walked her mother to the front door.

"I just can't believe you actually wanted to go to the beach," Mrs. Jahns said, puzzled. "When your dad and I took you years ago, you hated it. You'd only sit on the blanket or on our laps. You hated the sand. You'd scream if any got on your bathing suit. Daddy would try to coax you to at least put your feet in the water but you wouldn't have any part of it."

"I don't remember that."

"Of course you don't. You were three or four years old." Mrs. Jahns paused by the door. "Anyway, to calm you and let us have a moment's peace, Aunt Margie would walk with you along the boardwalk. To think that was fifteen years ago. Where has the time gone?"

Mrs. Jahns sighed. She usually didn't like bringing up the past.

"Well, getting back to reality, the boys ate already. Make sure they go to bed by ten. They're in the living room watching T.V. I left some macaroni in the refrigerator if you get hungry."

"Thanks, Mom"

Mrs. Jahns kissed her daughter's forehead.

"You don't know how wonderful it is to know I have a college-aged daughter who's home on a Saturday night. I see everyone boozing it up in my restaurant then driving home. When you were out with the twins, I always worried about the drunks on the road. Good night, dear. I'll see you around midnight."

Julia looked out the window until her mother's car disappeared down the street. Then she went to find her brothers.

CHAPTER EIGHT

Before long, June days turned into July. An oppressive heat wave tormented the east coast. It was so hot at night, the crickets stopped chirping.

"These are the dog days of summer," Aunt Margie would complain. "Oh how I love New Jersey! All my fan does is blow the hot air around."

"I sure wish we had an air conditioner," Mrs. Jahns responded, sitting on her sister's porch swishing a paper fan in front of her face. "This weather makes me wish I had moved to North Dakota with Wes."

"Even North Dakota has two miserably hot months," her sister replied. "And the rest of the year, you feel you're in an ice box. Where's Julia today?"

"She's at her job. She said her boss has the air conditioning on all the time. She even had to bring her sweater to work."

"I heard from the boys that she's not seeing those twins anymore. I never did like those two. Or their mother, for that matter."

"They've changed a lot the past year or so. They rarely go to church and their mother is constantly making excuses for them. I hear Clara is smoking again."

"That's how she keeps her skinny figure. Those girls of her sure don't have her shape."

"They have her face but they have their father's shape. They would be nicer looking if they just smiled more."

"Well, I'm glad my niece got some sense and rid herself of them. I'm sure at the college she has a wider bunch of people from which to pick companions."

"She seems more confident and peaceful these days," Mrs. Jahns replied. "Whoever she is spending time with, I'm glad to see a change in her. To me, her happiness is all that matters."

* * *

Julia sat at her desk in the law office, relishing the cool temperature. Eight hours spent here would not be a problem! The previous summer, when she had worked at Roote's with the twins, the store's air-conditioning system had frequently gone out. Jenny and Laine would drive to the YWCA after quitting time, jumping in the water to cool off. They were never anxious to return to their small, hot apartment.

"Wish we had a house," Jenny used to say. She would look at Julia with a pout.

"My house is really a cottage, Jenny."

"It's still a house. You own it."

"But the four of us are always on top of each other."

"And you have a back yard. Our mother said your mother is so lucky to have that yard. Your brothers can play outside. When we were their age, we played in a concrete parking lot."

"I guess I'm just lucky my mom didn't let my dad take the house when he left."

"That's true. I don't think our dad would have ever done that, would he, Laine? It wouldn't even occur to him to try to put his daughters out of their home."

On and on it went. Julia could not wait till they would depart so she could have peace. She never accompanied them to the pool. Both girls were athletic and accomplished swimmers. Julia was not. Her friends also enjoyed flirting with the male lifeguards. They would amuse everyone at Roote's the next day with exaggerated stories of their exploits.

As Julia thought back to that previous summer, she wondered if the twins had gotten summer jobs. Like herself, when they were out of school, finances were tight and they needed to work. A few days earlier, Julia had talked on the phone to Mary Lou and Pammy. Both said they missed her and wanted to know how she was doing. They did not mention the twins. The subject of the broken friendship was not broached, much to Julia's relief. On one occasion Mary Lou had asked Julia is she still planned to work in the English Department when school was back in session. Her queries led Julia to wonder how much her friends knew about her relationship with Aiden.

Back in May when classes had ended, Julia had given Aiden her office phone number but he never called. He said he preferred for her to get in touch with him. She had put the piece of paper with his phone number inside her wallet. It was a comfort to her, knowing it was there. She never questioned why he did not want to call her. She sensed he felt uneasy when she mentioned her friends or family knowing anything about him. The mysteriousness of their friendship added to the intrigue so she did not protest.

Looking at the law office calendar one late July morning, Julia realized Aiden's birthday was the following week. *July 30th --- I remember he said he'd be forty-five on that day!* She could not believe the summer was halfway over.

I have to buy him a present, she thought, *and it has to be something special*. Aiden always told her he thought birthdays were foolishness. "A reminder that death is that much closer," he would say. Julia dismissed his words. She wanted to make a fuss over him. Her family had always been in a celebratory state of mind as far as birthdays were concerned. "The happiest days of my life were when my three children were born," her mother would tell her. "And I will always celebrate those days, no matter how old my children get."

Browsing through a gift shop soon after, Julia noticed a display of small ceramic birds. She knew Aiden was hardly a knickknack collector but the urge to buy him a bird was overpowering. Didn't he once say his mother loved birds? And that he himself would like to be reincarnated as a bird? Her eyes were drawn to an eight-inch brown bird with a sharply pointed beak. The bird's breast had a black "vee" over painted yellow feathers, its upperparts dark brown, intertwined with black streaks.

"I'd like to buy this one, please," Julia said to a salesgirl.

The woman removed the piece from the glass shelf, wrapping it in tissue paper.

"A beautiful choice," she said to Julia, placing it gently in a box.

"It really is. Could you gift wrap it too?"

"Of course. Is it for a birthday?"

"Yes. Please pick out paper that isn't too flowery."

The salesgirl found dark blue paper and wrapped the package. Handing it to Julia, she smiled.

"By the way, do you realize we have all fifty state birds?"

"What?" Julia asked.

"In the back room. We have all fifty, one for each state. We only display a few due to lack of room."

"Then which state did I just buy?"

"Excuse me?"

"Which bird am I?"

"Let me look."

The salesgirl picked up the tag she had cut off and read the reverse side. She handed it to Julia.

"You're the meadowlark."

* * *

"What is this?"

Aiden saw a small box sitting on his desk. He glanced at his watch. How could it be ten o'clock so soon? He had arrived at school that morning, late for a meeting. His car, once again, had not started. Annoyed, he had waited half an hour for his mechanic. Running through the parking lot, he had dropped his briefcase, scattering papers. What more could go wrong? Walking down the main corridor at Raleigh, he noticed the stifling temperature. Once again, the school had lost its air-conditioning.

He called a secretary over and pointed to his desk.

"I don't know, Dr. Hunter," the woman said. "It was a delivery from a gift shop."

Aiden thanked her and then shut his door. He stared at the box for several minutes. A sudden brisk knock made him jump.

"Come in."

The door opened and he was surprised to see Sandee standing there. He ignored most of the support staff but he especially disliked this woman. He thought her voice too loud, her mannerisms too exaggerated and her dress inappropriate for an academia setting. That she disliked him as well was evident in her expression. She did not greet him but walked over to his desk, handing him a manila folder.

"What's this?"

"Your signature's needed on these forms," Sandee said. "They're to renew the work-study students. I noticed you forgot to sign an approval for Julia Jahns."

She emphasized the last two words with a bit of a sneer.

Aiden ignored her tone, looking around his desk for a pen.

"Julia Jahns," Sandee said. "I do remember that girl when she first signed up to work here. She stressed to me she *really* wanted to work in the English department. I wonder if you'd like to transfer her to another area. Professor Varnerum said the English department could save money by letting one student go. There's not enough work to keep her busy."

Aiden looked down at the paperwork.

"Is that so? Professor Varnerum has not relayed those thoughts to me."
He got out his pen and signed the slips.

* * *

Julia sat at her desk in the law firm office, sorting business cards and
opening mail. The phone rang, startling her.

"It's me, Mary Lou. Long time no talk! How are you Jules?"

"Fine. Good to hear from you. Can't talk long, I'm at work."

"I know. I just wanted to tell you that you have to stop by Raleigh and
sign a paper so you can work there next semester. Laine and Jenny were
talking about it when we were out dancing the other night. I know they won't
call you to let you know."

"Thanks, Mary Lou." Julia did not tell her that she had signed the
paperwork on the Saturday she had been with Aiden Hunter. "That was very
thoughtful of you."

"Glad I could help. By the way, a bit of gossip: Jenny is seeing Craig
again."

"No kidding! Is that stupid or what? Didn't he run off on her when he
thought he got her pregnant?"

"Yes he did. But you know her. She's crazy about him. I don't know what
she sees in such a shallow jerk. I know he's just using her. He makes fun of
her behind her back. His sister is in one of my classes and we talk. Believe
me, he doesn't like Jenny."

"So they're just….."

"Yeah, she's sleeping with him. He's using her for sex. What's happened to
that girl? She went from this innocent little creature last summer to practically
a streetwalker."

Mary Lou paused.

"You know, Jules, they were never good friends to you. The twins, I
mean. They were constantly saying they wanted you to date Lou but I heard
Jenny once say if you got a boyfriend before she did, or got engaged, she'd
really be mad."

"I know. It's nothing new."

"Well in a way, I hope you do. I hope you get married before they do. Or
at least find your true love. You've always been very nice to me and a good
friend."

"Thanks, Mary Lou. It's not that I'm ignoring you guys, it's just that I've been very busy with my life."

"Another thing before I hang up." Mary Lou lowered her voice. "Don't want to upset you but something's going on with that Sandee Dee person. She's got it in for Professor Hunter. I know you work for him and like him. The twins are friends with Sandee so I hear stuff. Did you know Louis Merlowe is her *nephew*?"

"Sandee's nephew? Are you kidding?"

"No. Apparently he isn't at Raleigh to take classes. I did think it was weird having a twenty-six year old man going to our school. I mean, didn't he finish college years ago? Apparently he is hanging around because he's having an affair with someone on staff."

"Louis Merlowe? The guy they were pushing on me?"

"Yeah, Sandee hadn't told the twins who his lover is but it's something shocking because Sandee is apparently on the warpath and trying to get the staff member fired."

"It can't be one of the secretaries, they're all middle-aged women."

"I don't know who it is. Maybe it's a professor. But I think the whole thing is strange. Why would Louis act like he wanted to date *you* when he's been in love with someone else?"

"Why is she mad at Professor Hunter?"

"Don't know. Maybe it's someone he can fire but won't. He's head of the English department so he has power. The whole thing is crazy."

"Gotta go, Mary Lou. But thanks for the information. And please call me again."

Julia slowly put the phone down. A cold chill went up her spine.

* * *

Something told Julia to go to Raleigh College. It was a strong inner urging which she could not shake. Many times she felt it was God pushing her to do something. Telling her boss she had to leave early, she grabbed her purse and hurried to her car. If she drove fast enough, she could get to the school before the summer staff left for the day.

Not stopping to lock her vehicle, she ran through the parking lot and into the building where the registrar had her office.

Another female staff member was sitting at Sandee's desk.

"I'm sorry," Julia said, out of breath. "I am not sure if I have to sign something to be able to work next semester. Is Sandee still here?"

"Hold on," the woman told her. "You look like a house on fire. Take a second to catch your breath, dear. Mrs. Dee will be back in a minute."

Julia was about to reply when she was interrupted by a loud laugh. Sandee had returned with another secretary but she did not yet see Julia.

"He's a strange one, all right," Sandee said to her companion. "That box is still on his desk, unopened."

Her coworker chuckled and went on down the hallway.

Oh heavens, Julia thought. *I wonder if they're talking about my gift!*

Julia had been looking forward to the weekend when Aiden would mention he had received her ceramic bird. The shop had been told to deliver it to him at the college.

Sandee suddenly noticed Julia and said no more. Her expression became subdued. The other secretary left the room, leaving the two of them alone.

"How are you, Julia?" Sandee said. Her tone was chilly.

"Fine," Julia replied. "I just stopped in to sign my work-study form."

"For this September? It's already been signed and approved. Perhaps you forgot you had signed it."

"Oh really?" Julia feigned confusion. "I guess I did. Sorry. I've been working at a law firm this summer and have been very forgetful."

"No problem."

Julia stood there, wondering what to say next.

"Can I help you with anything else?" Sandee asked. "We're closing in about fifteen minutes."

Before she could respond, another person appeared in the doorway.

Louis Merlowe!

Sandee's mouth dropped open, then she quickly shut it.

Louis, his face red and white-blond hair tousled, looked from Julia to Sandee and back again. His hands were shaking and his aqua eyes bright. Was it tears she saw?

"Oh, oh, I was just leaving," Sandee stuttered. "Time's about up. Yes, young man, what can I help you with?"

Louis, confused, frowned slightly and shook his head.

"Sorry. Wrong office. I'll just --- I'm gonna leave. And, and, why, hello, Julia."

"Hello, Louis."

The three of them stood frozen, not knowing what to do. Julia made the first move.

"I wanted to check on something in Professor Hunter's office before I left," she said.

Louis's face turned crimson. Sandee looked at him and scowled. She turned to Julia, her eyes cold.

"I'm sorry but that is not allowed. In fact, I'm sure his office is locked."

"I had something delivered to him and I wanted to make sure it got there," Julia said, surprising herself. It was if she were out of her body again, looking down at herself as she acted out a role.

"And what was that?"

"A small box. It was from a gift shop. It --- it is a birthday gift."

She noticed Louis's hands trembling at his side. His head was down and Sandee shot him a warning stare.

"Oh my, we give our professors birthday presents?" Sandee said. *"How nice is that.* Why, I haven't seen that done in the twenty years I've worked here. I do believe I did see a box on Dr. Hunter's desk earlier. He had not yet opened it. In fact, he acted like it wasn't even there."

Julia ignored Sandee's sarcasm. Smiling, she said, "I'm so glad it got there in time! Thank you so much for letting me know. Now I can rest easy. It's always a good thing when a birthday gift arrives in time especially when it's for someone who deserves something wonderful."

She left the room, but not without seeing the scowl on Sandee's face.

* * *

The following evening Julia sat on the worn out sofa in her living room, engrossed in a book. Her mother was at work, her two brothers having gone to her aunt's for the night. She stopped her reading every few minutes to take a sip of iced tea, relishing the quiet. It was so hot inside the house she had stuck her head under the bath tub faucet to get her hair wet. Without toweling it dry, she let the water drip down onto her tee-shirt. A large fan at her feet blew directly at her body but no matter what she did, she felt cranky and overheated.

I'm spoiled now, working in a cool law office, she thought. When she got a fulltime job, the first thing she was going to buy her mother was an air conditioner.

The phone rang, yanking her out of her reverie. Annoyed, she went into the kitchen to answer it.

"Hello?" she said, expecting to hear Aunt Margie or Ned's voice.

"Is this Julia?"

The female voice sounded familiar but Julia could not place it.

"Yes. Who's this?"

"I'm sorry to bother you at home but this is Mrs. Dee from the college."

A large knot started to form in Julia's stomach. She immediately thought of one word: trouble.

"I spoke to your mother a while ago," Sandee said.

"Yes she told me. Actually that was very annoying of you. And nervy."

"I'm sorry but I felt I had to. Your mother sure seems to put a lot of faith in you, Julia. Don't break that faith. I'm a mother too. If she knew about your relationship with your professor, she'd want it to stop."

"I don't know what you've heard but there's nothing going on."

"I think there is. And you really should know more about Dr. Hunter. He's not what you think. He's a closet homosexual. He goes to gay bars in the city on weekends. This is not idle gossip, Julia dear. He's been seen."

Sandee's words felt like dirty trash with the stench emanating into the phone line and into Julia's nostrils. She wanted to gag, push it away, run from the stink, but she could not hang up the phone.

"That --- isn't --- true."

She felt as if the breath were being knocked out of her.

"I know it's hard for you to hear but he's been seen," Sandee said. "Until now, I thought it was just talk. I was told he picks up different men, never the same person. He tries to go incognito. Someone I know recognized him and he denied he was Aiden Hunter. But he was. He is living a double life."

"Who is this person who told you this?"

"You'd be shocked if I told you. As I was shocked. I can't say who it was. But it's true. Professor Hunter is a very sick and disturbed individual."

Her voice softened.

"I'm truly sorry. I know you harbor a fondness for him and frankly I can't understand it. I've never liked the man. But I just don't think you know what you're doing. I also don't know what he's doing. If you ask me, he's pathetic. You're a young girl, your whole life is ahead of you. Don't have any more to do with him."

"I don't believe it."

Julia's hands trembled. She was glad Sandee could not see her reaction.

"I'm sorry, but I had to inform you. I didn't want to say anything to you with that young man in my office yesterday."

"You mean your nephew, Louis Merlowe?"

"I guess you found out about Lou. Yes, he is my nephew. I've basically raised him since he was ten years old."

"I don't care if he's your nephew. I don't care who he is. Professor Hunter is my friend and I do not have to listen to this. And I don't want to talk about this anymore." Julia suddenly felt anger rising up inside her. *How dare this miserable woman intrude on my life!* "You have no idea what Aiden Hunter is like. I resent you calling me and I resent the accusations. Please never call me again."

Julia slammed down the receiver.

Well, Mary Lou was sure right about Sandee making trouble for Aiden, she thought after she had calmed down. *But what a lowdown way to go about it.*

It was all beginning to make sense. Sandee, protective of her nephew, wanted to get someone fired at the college. Someone Louis had been sleeping with. The affair ended badly and now Louis wanted revenge. Sandee felt she had enough power to make that happen. She knew Aiden was on the committee to hire and fire. If Aiden refused to dismiss someone because of a sexual entanglement, he would be stirring up Sandee's wrath.

And what better way to cause trouble for Aiden than to accuse him of being gay. He's a single man in his forties, so what better way to start a rumor?

The more Julia thought about it, the more serene she became.

Aiden wasn't gay! He loved her and she felt his love when she was with him. *Gay men hate women*, she told herself. *Not that I know any gay men personally.* But she had always heard that homosexual men chose other men because of their disgust with females.

"Aiden doesn't hate females," Julia said aloud. "And he's not the least bit effeminate."

The more she thought about it, the angrier she became.

Sandee Dee is going to be sorry she ever started this, Julia thought. *She has no idea who she is dealing with.*

She was to see Aiden the following day. Should she tell him what was going on? No, better to keep quiet. It was not worth upsetting him. Julia felt confident she could handle Sandee Dee and Louis Merlowe on her own.

Satisfied with her mental conclusions, she went back to the living room to finish her book. But first, she unplugged the telephone.

* * *

That Saturday, alone with Aiden in an outdoor café, Julia toyed with the napkin in front of her.

"You are very quiet today," Aiden remarked. "I was going to say maybe the heat got you but that oppressive heatwave we've had seems to have lifted. I believe it's only 79 degrees today."

"Yes, it is so much cooler out."

"You look sad. Is something the matter?"

Julia kept her eyes down.

"Just wanted to know if you --- did you get something in the mail?"

"Oh, yes. I forgot to thank you. Is that why you're not talking much? That was thoughtful of you to remember my birthday even though you know my feelings on such matters. And the bird choice was --- well, it was fitting."

Julia felt her eyes fill with tears.

"Whatever is wrong?"

Aiden reached for her hand but she stood up.

"I just can't talk about it. I just can't."

"Please sit down. You don't have to talk about anything. Why are you upset? Here, let's leave and go for a walk."

He put money on the table, took her arm, and led her to the sidewalk.

"There's a park nearby. Let's go there."

They crossed the street and walked several blocks in silence.

"I sent you that present in your office," Julia said after awhile.

"I know you did. Is that why you're dismayed? That I didn't tell you I received it?"

"No."

"I certainly wasn't going to open anything on campus and give those secretaries something to wag their tongues over."

"So you think the secretaries are gossips?"

"Yes, all the female staff members are like bleating sheep. Not just the secretaries. Nothing going on in their dull, miserable lives so they have to mind everyone else's business."

"And you think sometimes they spread lies?"

"I believe they do. What on earth got you into such a feverish mood? Put those battle-axes out of your mind."

Suddenly Julia felt a torrent of emotion. She loved him, she hated him, and she wanted to pummel him with her fists.

Instead, she stopped walking. He looked at her in confusion.

"What?" he said.

Before he could respond, she turned and threw herself into his arms, sobbing. Caught off guard, for a moment he did not know what to do. He put his arms around her, patting her back. *Was the ceramic bird the cause of this? Was she hurt because I didn't mention it sooner? Or was it because I didn't acknowledge its origin? I certainly knew it was a meadowlark.*

He became aware of her body against him. He lowered his head and brushed his lips against the top of her hair. She smelled like honeysuckle. He closed his eyes. A faint memory stirred but he did not recognize the source.

My darling, he wanted to way. *I love you so.* But he could not.

He did not know why the words lie frozen on his lips. They had screamed to him from his heart. But he could not say them. He let her cry while he remained silent.

"I'm sorry," she finally said, pulling away from him. "I don't know what's the matter with me."

Aiden looked at her, his heart pounding in his chest, a longing to sweep her back in his arms, kiss her lips, enveloped him. As suddenly as the feeling began, it left him. He felt the wall come down, the divide he could not penetrate. His thwarted desire for her now revolted him. He had wanted her for a brief moment but then his need sickened him. He turned away from her, desperately wanting a drink. He felt he had been about to violate something sacred.

He was ashamed.

"What's the matter, Aiden?"

It was the first time she had ever spoken his first name.

"Don't call me that."

Aiden turned and walked several steps away from her. She was so startled by his abrupt change of tone that she stopped crying.

"I'm sorry. I didn't mean to ---"

"You've never called me that."

"But it's your name."

"I know. It doesn't seem right."

"I'm sorry."

Her reddened, tear-streaked face looked pitiable. *Why did I say that to her?* He suddenly hated himself. *What is wrong with me?*

"I'm sorry, too. I don't know why I just said that."

"What do you want me to call you?"

"I don't know. Aiden is fine. Call me Aiden."

"You have never called me by my name."

"I haven't, have I. I've only called you by your surname."

"It's so weird. We've been friends for months. I had trouble saying your name until now."

"I have a problem with that, too. I don't know why."

"It's okay. You can keep calling me Miss Jahns."

"Call me anything you want. Forgive me for my outburst."

She wanted to hug him again but sensed something had changed. The embrace had frightened him. She could not understand it. She could not understand their relationship.

"I think I should go home now," Julia said.

She wanted to be alone, to sort things out in her mind.

"If that's what you want."

He didn't argue with her, did not beg her to stay. *Why?*

He drove her back to her car at the university parking lot. He watched her drive away. Never had he felt lonelier.

* * *

The road was dark, the one street light by the apartment house broken. Fumbling with the keys, he became furious when he could not immediately find the right one. He did not like this. Normally he came home alone. He did not like anyone in his space, upsetting his things, looking around. This time he had relented. Mutual attraction like this rarely happened anymore; he could not let such an opportunity slip through his fingers.

It would be a welcome interlude. He had not gone into the city in a while. He had not felt such depression for a long time. Drinking alone did not help on this occasion. He had to leave his apartment, had to change his pattern. Too many people knew him at that other bar. It could prove to be a nightmare. He liked the anonymity at this new place. The clientele looked more upscale. It wasn't long before he noticed a pair of eyes watching him. They burned into his own with a fiery light. He lit a cigarette and ordered a martini. The flaming gaze remained on him. After a few moments, he felt a hand on his shoulder. Another drink was bought. Then another. The alcohol dimmed his thinking, at the same time inflaming his lust. His depression began to evaporate into a haze.

Several hours later they were back at his apartment. The young man started to turn on the light as he entered the room behind him.

"Don't touch that. Don't touch anything."

"How am I supposed to see where I'm going?"

He led him into the back room. A nightlight was on, otherwise they would have stumbled into total darkness.

"Not much for ambiance, are you?"

When he did not respond, the young man shrugged. These older guys were so set in their ways. This one appeared especially fidgety. Kind of a grouch.

The young man wanted to turn on the bedroom light.

"No. Leave it."

He obeyed, leaning back on the bed, watching him.

"You like it pitch black, huh?"

Again he got no response. He started to unbutton his shirt, watching the older guy go into the bathroom. When he emerged a few moments later, he did a strange thing. He went over to the nightstand and threw a towel over a knickknack.

"I don't think that bird's going to fly away anytime soon."

The young man laughed at his own remark but was met by silence.

He could tell this middle-aged guy had absolutely no sense of humor.

* * *

August came. One rainy morning, Ruth Jahns picked up the ringing telephone. She had a feeling it would be her sister and she knew why she was calling.

"Hi, Margie," she said. "Let me guess what you're going to say...."

"It's that time of year," Marge replied. "Julia's going to be nineteen soon."

"You always call a week before to see what we're doing."

"It's a ritual. Nineteen isn't a milestone but it's my favorite niece and I want to take her out to dinner."

"Favorite niece? Only niece!"

"My almost-daughter, since I only have a son."

"Speaking of your son, please tell Neddie the car is running great. So glad he fixed it up for her."

"I'll tell him. And you tell Julia we'll take her out to Rodgers for dinner on Wednesday. It's not far, it's off Route 11. And of course you're coming too."

"Should I bring the boys?"

"Of course. I'm paying, so I don't want to hear another word about it."

"Thank you."

"Oh, and I have a surprise. Nothing big. Just something that might make a difference."

"For Julia?"

"Yes. Maybe for you, too."

* * *

Julia sat behind her desk at the law office, thinking about her last outing with Aiden Hunter. Their day had ended on a sour note, with her crying, Aiden reacting strangely and then her demand to go home. She felt guilty.

It had been four days since she had seen him and she missed him. Usually she didn't think of him during the week, assured she would be with him on Saturday. But today was Wednesday and she felt a pang when she thought of him.

Maybe I miss him so much now because I told him I wanted to go home, she thought. *Maybe I hurt his feelings.*

She took out the slip with his phone number from her wallet. After staring at it for a few moments, she decided to call him.

Then the strangest thing happened. The phone rang. And it was Aiden.

It's telepathy! she thought when she picked up and heard his voice. *God had to be in this! Why else would he call at that very second? He said he would never call!*

"Hello," he said. "Millicent?"

"What?"

"I've decided to call you Millicent."

"Aiden, is that you? Are you drinking?"

"Not at all. I'm sorry to call you at work. Is it a bad time?"

"No. No one's here. *Millicent?*"

"You said I never call you by your name. I decided from now on I will call you Millicent."

"That's an old lady name. I don't know if I like it."

"It's a regal name. It's what a baroness would call herself."

"Now I know you've been drinking."

"I assure you I have not."

"What made you change my name? Why would you call me such a name?"

"It came to me in a dream….no, seriously, it just came to me. I think it's a beautiful name and that is what I am going to call you. Starting now."

"Okay......."

Julia wished she could smell his breath over the phone.

Millicent! Of all names!

"Anyway, I was also calling to tell you it's your birthday soon."

"Yes, I'll be nineteen. Next Wednesday. My last teen-aged year."

"I have bought you a gift."

"That's very thoughtful."

"I shall give it to you Saturday. If indeed you meet me Saturday."

"Of course I will. We meet every Saturday."

"After our last meeting, I wasn't sure you wanted to see me."

"Let's forget about last Saturday."

"Agreed."

"So you're okay?"

"Yes, of course.

"See you then. See you Saturday."

* * *

Saturday came quickly. Julia met Aiden at Lee University, as usual, glad the heatwave had lifted. It was a cool, sunny day. Cool, that is, for August in New Jersey.

"Let's walk to the park near River's Edge Road," he said when she arrived. "There's a free play starting at one thirty. A love story, which I'm sure you would enjoy. But first we can get something to eat."

"Okay," she said, wondering where he had hidden her gift.

"And I will give you your present during lunch," he said, as if reading her mind.

He took her hand in his.

"So you will be nineteen soon," Aiden said as they walked together.

"Yes. But I've been a legal adult since last year."

"Oh yes, a legal adult!"

He chuckled, and Julia was glad to see him in a good mood.

"Many people actually marry at age nineteen," she said. "At least in my mom's generation they did."

"Quite true. Did you know my own mother was married at age sixteen?"

"Sixteen! I can't imagine it."

"And my father was eighteen. Years ago it wasn't that unusual. Especially for country folk. Not much to do in Nebraska except farm and reproduce."

Julia laughed.

"I want to know something," Aiden said a few minutes later. "I don't know how to say it."

"Yes?"

"Last Saturday. When you were, so….distressed. When you flung yourself at me…."

"When I hugged you?"

"Yes."

He looked uncomfortable.

"What about it?"

"Did you --- did you expect more from me?"

"More from you? What do you mean?"

"Was I, did I do the right thing? Was I what you needed?"

"Needed? Why of course. You're my friend and you ---"

Aiden shook his head.

"I'm not saying it right. That's not what I meant."

They stopped walking.

"Do you love me?"

The question shocked her. Again, she felt like she was out of her body, floating upward, and watching herself down below.

"Yes."

She heard the word come out of her mouth. *But did she mean it?*

I want to say I love him when I'm away from him, she thought. *But when I'm with him, I have no desire to say it at all.* Until now. But not really. She only said yes to his question. She could not actually say the three words.

"So you say you love me," Aiden continued. "But are you in love with me?"

"In love?"

"Yes. Did you want to --- oh, never mind."

Julia felt confused.

"I just told you so," she said. "So that means a person would be in love with you. What's the difference?"

There was a long pause.

"Is there a difference, Aiden?"

"Hmmmmmm?"

"Are you in love with me?"

"What do you think?"

"I think you are. Even though you said you didn't believe in love."

"I said that?"

"Don't be silly. You know you did."

He smiled and his smile reminded her of something from long ago --- what was it? Oh yes, the Mona Lisa.

Has he again been drinking? she wondered. But as she watched him, he seemed sober. She had never been around anyone before who drank often but she was learning to observe the signs.

"I feel stronger when I'm with you," she said later when they sat in a café near the university. "Since we have been together, I feel so different."

"I'm glad. I feel happier with you, too."

"I used to worry all the time. About jobs, about school, about my friends. Now I feel I don't care. It's like I've been set free."

"That is good to hear."

"I didn't know how much more of my life I could have taken."

He took her hand in both of his.

Soon after, as they finished their meal, Aiden reached into his pocket and pulled out a gold box.

"Here," he said, handing her the box. "Take this. It is your gift."

She held the battered box, turning it over in her hands.

"I'm sorry I did not wrap it. I didn't think it needed anything else. Open it up."

Julia lifted the lid. Under a wad of worn cotton was a piece of jewelry. A sterling silver pendant with a floral etching hung from a silver chain. She lifted it into the air and held it close to her eyes so she could study the design.

"This is beautiful," she said. "It's like an antique."

"It most likely is."

"Where on earth did you find something like this?"

"It was my grandmother's. She had it made for my mother's birthday. It is really very old."

"Your mother?"

"Yes, but my mother died before my grandmother could give it to her. Do you see the etching?"

"Yes, they look like flowers."

"I think they are dandelions. I believe that's why my grandmother chose this pendant. She told me my mother was always happiest when her children picked dandelions for her."

Julia was awestruck.

"It's beyond being beautiful. It's amazing."

"I know. I want you to have it."

Suddenly Julia felt tears come to her eyes.

"It's your mother's. I can't take it."

"I want you to have it. My mother never even saw it."

Julia cradled the pendant in her hands.

"It's for your birthday and it is my gift to you," Aiden repeated. "It's now yours."

"I can't possibly take something that's been in your family for years."

"You will hurt my feelings if you don't take it."

Julia looked up at him and made a face.

"Now I know you're being silly."

She undid the clasp and put it around her neck.

"But shouldn't this stay in your family?"

"Why do you say that?"

"Shouldn't Guenther's daughter have this? It was her grandmother's."

Julia was surprised to see his expression darken.

"No," he said. "The pendant was given to me to dispose of as I wish."

"Don't get angry, Aiden. I'm honored to have it. It's beautiful and knowing it's from you makes it that more special. I just don't feel ---"

She paused, shaking her head.

"I'm honored. Thank you so much."

He helped her with the clasp and the pendant hung from her neck.

They left the eatery in silence, and it occurred to her that Aiden had not called her Millicent once.

CHAPTER NINE

"You're going where?"

"To Florida. Just for two weeks. That was the surprise my Aunt Margie told us about. Her mother-in-law died last year and left my aunt a lot of money. She wants to celebrate and take my family with her to Florida. She said it's for my nineteenth birthday but it's really for all of us."

"Oh?"

"It's only for two weeks. We're flying down tomorrow."

Julia's last conversation with Aiden before she left for Florida played itself over in her memory for the next several days. August was winding down, school would soon be resuming. The days, though hot and humid, were already getting shorter.

Julia had been spending her weekdays at work, half her weekends with Aiden Hunter. They ate lunch together every Saturday and Julia could tell Aiden loved the arrangement. He would sometimes gaze at her without saying a word.

"What are you smiling at?" she once said.

"At you. I like you being here with me. I'm not so lonely."

"What did you do before I came?"

"I suppose I just tried to ignore how lonely I was."

Then came Aunt Margie's offer to take Julia away for two weeks.

Aiden scowled all through their meal.

"It's not long. It's only two weeks," she told him, sitting at a diner in Tilletsen. "I can't say no and not go. My mother and aunt would be crushed."

Julia felt flattered that Aiden was angry.

"I just don't like it," he said. "Something about it rubs me the wrong way."

"Well, I've never had a real vacation," Julia said. "We've always been too poor. I've never even been on an airplane."

"What about your job?"

"It's ending soon anyway. My boss understands. He was shocked I had never even been out of the state of New Jersey."

"Florida is hot, buggy and totally uninteresting," he replied. "A flat state containing nothing but everglades and alligators."

"You're in a good mood!"

"I'm sorry, but you can't expect me to be pleased about this."

"It's only two weeks. I will be back."

"Will you?"

"Of course."

As they said goodbye that day, Aiden reached for her hand and squeezed it. "I shall see you soon."

* * *

During the flight to Florida, Ruth Jahns asked her daughter why she was so quiet.

"My first plane ride; I'm a little scared," Julia fibbed. She was not at all frightened; she was thinking about Aiden and wondering if he would forget her in two weeks. Part of her was worried, but another part was oddly indifferent.

What's wrong with me?

"I wonder if Julia has a boyfriend she's not told you about," Aunt Margie whispered to her sister later that day. "She looks upset."

"It could be. I'm not asking any questions. I know she goes out every Saturday but doesn't say who she's with. I figure she'll tell me eventually."

"Knowing Julia, it's a boyfriend she left behind. And I bet he's someone special. I see her as a pastor's wife someday. Is she still going to the same church?"

"No, she told me she's looking for a new one. The Murdens still show up at St. John's. Julia's trying to avoid places they go."

"Maybe that's a good thing. Those twins' personalities were too overpowering for my taste. But if I know my niece, she'll set her sights on a fine young man. She's not one to settle."

"Julia doesn't know this but Clara Murden called me a few weeks ago, crying her eyes out. Jenny had gotten pregnant a few months back. She miscarried. I heard it was a boy she only dated once or twice."

"It's unbelievable. Those girls were always in church. Maybe Jenny's just gotten in with a wild crowd."

"I think so. The more I hear about Jenny lately, the more shocked I am."

"It's case of 'like mother, like daughter.' Wasn't Clara Murden three months along when she married Chet?"

"I don't like to gossip but yes, that's exactly the way it was. I don't think she ever told her girls the story but she told me. Chet was quite infatuated with Lillian MacKay who was the prettiest girl in the class. Clara chased him anyway. Then after Chet found out she was having his baby, he felt obligated to marry her."

"A baby? Two babies. What a surprise to both of them."

"Clara had her cap set for Chet Murden and nothing was to get in her way. Well it didn't get her much, did it?"

"It certainly didn't."

"Sometimes I feel like telling Julia about that situation when those twins brag about their perfect father. They do it deliberately to make my daughter feel bad. I'd love for them to know the Chet Murden I've heard about. At least Julia's dad was in love with me when we got married. And our baby was made in love, not from a roll in the backseat of a car."

* * *

A few days after Julia had left for Florida, Aiden received a phone call from his brother.

"I have an old friend I've been corresponding with that lives in New York City, Aiden. I'm coming east tomorrow to see her. Remember Dorothy Sperry?"

"Vaguely."

"I'm sure you do. She lived in the old Petersen farmhouse when we were kids. Her family moved east her last year of high school. We had dated a few months in my junior year. I was quite enamored of her if you recall."

"Yes," Aiden said, though he did not remember.

"She contacted me and we've been keeping in touch, mostly by phone calls. She's asked me to fly out and see her. I'm taking an early morning flight."

"You're flying all the way here just to meet some woman for dinner?"

"Well, yes. To tell you the truth, I'm rather lonely. Dorothy's been a widow for five years. She's actually thinking about moving back to Nebraska. She heard of my divorce and —"

"Went in for the kill."

Guenther chuckled, not sure if Aiden was being playful or cynical.

"Anyway, I will stop by and see you if you're around."

"Yes, I'm here."

"Good. By the way, I went to see Aunt Berta in the old age home last week. She gave me an envelope full of photographs."

"Oh?"

"Apparently Father had given them all to his brother after our mother died. He didn't want them around. After Uncle Frank died last year, Aunt Berta found them when she cleaned out his desk. Lots of photos of Mother and a few of our brother George."

"Father gave them away? I am not surprised."

"I guess he couldn't stand being reminded of her. Anyway, to think in all these years, we never had more than a couple photos of Mother."

"Another act of Father's selfishness. He had two sons who would have appreciated those snapshots. Instead, he gives them to Frank."

"Who can fathom how people grieve? He was young, I suppose he didn't want to be reminded of her passing. Remember, they had lost a child five years earlier. Mother died at a very young age. Father had to deal with so much."

"I have but one photo of our mother."

"I know. Now we have many more. I have mailed them to you."

"As you wish."

"I have looked the photos over. It was heart wrenching and I felt tears come to my eyes. You know I am rarely emotional. I don't really remember our mother but somehow, seeing her likeness brought something back. A sadness. I noticed our brother George looked exactly like her. I also went through some correspondence. Uncle Frank saved everything. I'm not certain, Aiden, but it seems Mother's death was not the way we were told."

"What do you mean?"

"There were many letters between Father and Uncle Frank. From reading them, I discovered our mother was deeply melancholy. They didn't understand post-partum depression in those days. George's death happened during a period when Mother was suffering from the blues, apparently after your birth."

"So?"

"So here's a farmer's young wife, stuck in the house through a long, cold winter with a toddler who has just died. She has you, six months old, a colicky baby from what I read, who kept her up nights. Women in those days were supposed to be strong, they were of pioneer stock. Mother had no one to talk to. After giving birth to me, she couldn't get pregnant again. Or wouldn't, I'm not sure which. Father said they had wanted a big family. In his letters to his brother, he complains of her being cold to him. She then spends the next few years throwing herself into her two remaining sons' lives --- yours and mine. Apparently she had her good moments and bad moments. All culminating in that March day in 1936 when she decided she had enough."

Aiden was silent.

"I believe she committed suicide, Aiden."

"I don't believe it. Not for a minute." Aiden's voice was icy. "How dare you even say that. Leave it to Father, even in death, to tarnish her name. He knew someday we'd find these letters. You can believe what you want. I believe what our grandmother told us."

"Well I read the letters. If you want, I could mail you copies of them."

"I don't want copies. Father was a liar and I am sure he lied to his brother."

"Father and Uncle Frank found Mother's body. You were with her, screaming and holding on to her."

"I don't recall anything like that."

"Of course you don't. You were five. You most likely blocked it all out."

"Rubbish. I would certainly remember something like that."

"I don't know, Aiden. I don't know."

Guenther did not feel like arguing with his brother. Why add to his pain? He had always heard what a mama's boy Aiden had been. His mother had been taken from him at the height of the child's Oedipal attachment.

"Aiden, when you receive the photos, study them. Let me know who you think our mother looks like."

"You just told me she looked like George."

"Yes, she did. But I see a resemblance to someone else. Quite striking, in fact. Almost eerie. It might explain a lot."

"I don't know what you're talking about."

"Just promise to let me know what you think. I've mailed you about twenty-five photos. They are yours to keep."

Guenther decided to change the subject.

"Getting on to other things, how have you been?"

"Well."

"And how is Julia?"

"She is well."

"Is she visiting you this Saturday?"

"No, she's in Florida with her family."

"Oh, I see. Then you should come out to dinner with us. We're going early."

"No, thank you."

"Aiden, don't be stubborn. You should meet Dorothy. She used to teach college courses herself. You'd have a lot to talk about."

"I'm sorry, I might be meeting some friends in the city."

"If you change your mind, let me know. I'll be staying at the Minuteman Hotel. I'm sure you can get the number."

Guenther hung up the phone and frowned. Aiden sounded troubled. He knew his brother well enough to wonder if he would take Julia's absence as a rejection. The "friends in the city" remark was also disturbing. Guenther suspected Aiden's activities did not involve friendship. He said a quick prayer. Then he started to pack.

* * *

Aiden Hunter laid on the bed, out of breath, sweating, a drink in his hand.

"Don't spill that now."

He looked over at the young man, a smile on his face.

"I wouldn't worry about it. What did you pay for this room? Five dollars?"

"That's not the point."

"It's not exactly the Ritz."

"And you're not exactly Rock Hudson. But I love you anyway."

Aiden placed his glass on the nightstand.

"You always do that."

"Do what?" Aiden said.

"You never answer when I proclaim my love for you."

"Love is such a complicated word."

"I disagree. For me it's quite simple."

Aiden reached out and tousled the white-blond hair. The young man grabbed his hand and kissed it.

"So was it my note that did it?"

"Did what?"

"Don't be coy, Aiden, you know exactly what I mean. I don't believe you never read my note. And now here we are. So I assume my pleas and begging worked."

Aiden did not respond.

"Sometimes I think you're a cold man."

"There are things," Aiden said, "that you don't understand."

"I'm not understanding you now. And not to start an argument, but there's a lot of talk about your relationship with that work-study student. Not that I'm worried you're having sex with her. I'm probably the only one at Raleigh who knows it's purely platonic."

"I will not discuss her with you. That is a topic we are never to share."

"If I didn't know better, I'd be jealous."

The young man pouted, waiting for a reaction.

"Well? Should I be jealous?"

"No."

"Good. And I know you love me even though you won't admit it."

He did not wait for a response, but climbed into bed beside Aiden, knocking over the glass of gin in his impatience.

* * *

Dinner with Dorothy Sperry was delightful. Guenther Hunter hummed in his rental car the entire ten mile drive to his brother's apartment. He had phoned Aiden hours earlier but had gotten no response. He was not worried. If Aiden were not home, Guenther planned on staying overnight at a nearby motel. Tilletsen was seedy but Guenther, a farm boy at heart, had never been squeamish.

Realizing his brother treasured his privacy, Guenther knew he took a risk dropping by unannounced, especially during the evening. Aiden might be annoyed enough to refuse to answer the door. He glanced at his watch. It was nine thirty. There was a good chance Aiden would not be at home.

The front light was on as Guenther pulled up. Climbing the steps, he noticed the doorbell was out of order. He knocked on the door several times. Getting no response, he stood on the top step, debating whether to leave a note on the door. As he reached into his pocket to retrieve a pen, he heard a loud crash. It sounded like it was coming from inside the apartment. Guenther put his pen back and began to pound on the door.

"Aiden! Can you hear me?"

Several seconds went by and he turned the knob. To his surprise, the door opened. It was unlike Aiden to ever leave his apartment unlocked. It was a sketchy neighborhood even in the daylight hours.

Guenther stepped inside, switching on the light. His eyes blinked in the sudden brightness. A dark form lie huddled on the uncarpeted living room floor beside a broken glass lamp.

"Oh my God," Guenther said.

He ran for the telephone.

* * *

Julia sat in the hotel room watching her mother and aunt get her brothers ready for the beach.

"Are you sure you don't want to come with us?" Aunt Margie said. "It's going to be beautiful by the water."

"No thanks. I'm going to read awhile. I might go after four, when the sun isn't so intense."

"All right, dear. I'm glad you found those novels in the lobby. I know how you've always had your nose in a book."

Julia curled up on the loveseat in their spacious room, a cup of iced tea beside her. The air conditioner was on the highest setting. What could be better? She wondered what Aiden was doing. It had been the first Saturday in months that they had not been together.

* * *

"Are you a relative of Mr. Hunter's?"

Guenther stood to his feet as the doctor made his way over to him. His Styrofoam cup of now-cold coffee sloshed as he placed it on the table.

"Yes, I'm his brother. I'm a doctor as well. How is he doing?"

"He'll be fine. We sewed up his arm. Seventeen stitches."

"Thank goodness."

"He's lucky. He just missed an artery. You can go in and talk to him."

"Thank you, doctor."

"We did some blood work too. I'm sure everything is all right. Looks like he just had a little too much to drink."

Guenther said little on the ride home. Aiden sat in the passenger seat, eyes closed.

"It's too late for you to drive to New York," Aiden said when they pulled into his driveway. "Just stay here for the night."

Night? Guenther thought. *It's almost dawn.*

"I think I will."

Hours later, after spending an uncomfortable snooze on the sofa, Guenther glanced at his watch. His plane wasn't leaving for another eight hours. Going into the kitchen, he found Aiden sitting at the table sipping coffee.

"Lucky for you when you fell and knocked over that lamp, it took a slice out of your arm and not your head," Guenther said, yawning. "Think of the scar you'd have."

"It feels as if I've cracked open my skull. I have a throbbing headache."

"The coffee should help. It appears every time I come see you, there's a major problem."

"I didn't realize I had so much to drink."

"Oh, come now, Aiden, of course you did. How many times can you deny you have a problem?"

Aiden looked over at his brother with half-closed eyes.

"I have less of a problem than you'd like to imagine. I don't drink all the time."

"But when you do, you do it excessively. Therefore, you have a problem."

Guenther went over to the counter to pour himself a cup of coffee.

"So how was dinner with your old friend?"

"Actually, Aiden, we had a great time."

"I hope you're not in a hurry to get married again."

"Why would you think that? I most certainly am not."

Aiden rubbed his temples. The coffee was not helping.

"I can see you are in no condition to have a conversation with," Guenther said. "And on that note, I will finish my caffeine and take a shower. Then I will be on my way."

"Before you go, Guenther," Aiden said. "I wanted to ask you something."

Guenther gulped down his coffee then rinsed the cup in the sink.

"Oh, and what is that?"

"On the subject of marriage."

"My marriage?"

"No. I was thinking of ---"

Aiden paused.

"I was thinking of asking Miss Jahns to marry me."

Guenther stood still, the coffee cup and dish towel in his hand. He turned toward his brother.

"What did you just say?"

"You heard me."

Guenther walked over to Aiden and put his hand on his shoulder. He shook his head.

"You must have had a concussion."

"Don't be condescending."

"Condescending? I'm being realistic."

"Reality has never interested me."

"Aiden, you must not be thinking clearly."

"Skip the sarcasm. I'm sorry I brought it up."

"You can't be serious. Why, when you are sixty, this young girl will be only thirty-four. When you're seventy, she will be forty-four ---"

"I can do the math."

"You are friends, not lovers. There is no basis for a marriage. If she were crazy enough to marry you now, you'd have her gone in less than a year. And no doubt like most women, in a few years, she'd want children. Have you sat down and thought this out? Have you even hinted of this to her?"

Guenther shook his head.

"My God, Aiden, you can't even say her first name!"

"Stop screaming."

"I'm sorry."

There was a long pause and Guenther sighed.

"From all I understand about your relationship with this girl, I have very good advice," he said. "Please listen to it."

"And what is that?"

"I think you should definitely change Miss Jahns' last name to match yours."

"Oh, so you now agree that I should marry her?"

"Not at all. You should adopt her."

* * *

The strong Florida sun shone through the window of the family style restaurant. Julia studied the menu, trying to decide what to order. She had been in Florida for eight days and today she would return to New Jersey. She missed Aiden more than she thought she would. She was also bored. Never having liked the summertime, she did not enjoy humid temperatures that climbed into the hundreds. The climate was so uncomfortable, she didn't even want to leave the hotel room. And though she loved her aunt and mother, there was only so much of being around them constantly that she could take.

Her aunt could not understand why she wanted to go home. Julia fibbed and told her that her summer job might be jeopardized if she did not return.

After a discussion with Aunt Margie and her mother, they agreed she should fly home. Julia's family would remain in Florida for another week. Aunt Margie exchanged her ticket and after lunch, she would board a plane for Newark Airport. Home sweet home. Her cousin Ned, Margie's son, agreed to pick her up and drive her home.

"You only have that part-time job for another week or two and then you're back to college," Aunt Margie had said. "Does it matter if they fire you?"

"I promised I'd be there if they really needed me," Julia said. "I've been gone over a week. I really should keep my word. Mr. Shaw is swamped with work."

"Julia's as honest as the day is long," Mrs. Jahns said. "I understand, honey. That's why you're not only the best daughter but the best employee."

Aunt Margie had rushed to the lobby to make a phone call. When she returned, her eyes twinkled.

"Before you leave, Julia, we're all going to lunch."

"Looks like she's got something up her sleeve," Julia's mother remarked. "Your aunt never gets that excited over eating out."

At the airport, two hours before Julia's flight was to leave, Aunt Margie treated them to lunch.

"This is an all-you-can-eat place," Mrs. Jahns said. "We should have some of these in New Jersey. With two growing boys, this would be a godsend."

"Speaking of growing boys," Aunt Margie said, "a friend of Ned's might be stopping by. They were close buddies in college. His name is Steve Lundquist. He's taking graduate courses down here in Florida but he's originally from New Jersey. Do you remember him, Ruthie?"

Mrs. Jahns shook her head.

"He was that tall, thin kid with strawberry blond hair and glasses," Aunt Margie said. "I think you met him once. Anyway, he heard from Ned we were in town and said he'd try to drop in and say hello. I called him and told him we'd be eating here."

"Was that your call on the lobby phone?"

Aunt Margie rolled her eyes then winked at her sister. Julia caught them exchanging glances and sighed.

Are they trying to fix me up again?

"He's a fine Christian man," Aunt Margie said. "He's twenty-seven, a year older than Ned and works for an accounting firm. He took some time off to get his masters degree."

"Sounds like an ambitious fellow," Mrs. Jahns replied. "And a Christian too, you say?"

"He rents an apartment in Summers Point but Ned said he's saving for a house. He's very mature. And focused."

"So Ned still sees him?"

"They try to get together but Ned's been busy with that new girlfriend of his."

Julia rolled her eyes.

Ten minutes later a tall, slender man walked over to their table. His thick reddish blond hair hung near his collar, his clear blue eyes sparkled behind gold-rimmed glasses.

"Steve! How nice to see you."

Aunt Margie stood up and pulled out a chair.

"Everyone, this is Steve Lundquist, the young man I told you about. Steve, my family. Please join us."

Conversation continued and Julia noticed how comfortable Steve appeared around her family. He obviously knew Aunt Margie well. He ordered a cola and sat at their table for almost an hour.

"I have to be going," he said. "On my way to my part-time job. It was nice seeing you again, Mrs. Coppins."

Aunt Margie beamed.

"When you're back in Jersey, look us up, Steve. Don't be a stranger."

"I'm actually flying back home tomorrow," Steve said. "A friend of mine is getting married. Maybe I'll stop by and see if old man Ned is around."

"I'm sure he'd love that."

Steve turned to Julia.

"I hear you're flying back to New Jersey this afternoon."

"Yes," Aunt Margie said. "We're seeing her off."

"It was nice meeting you, Julia," Steve said, extending his hand. "Maybe we'll meet again."

Julia took his hand and felt a rush of heat. Steve's bright blue eyes looked into hers and she blushed.

Why am I turning red? she thought, irritated with herself. *I am certainly not interested in this guy.*

"When are you moving back north permanently?" Mrs. Jahns asked.

"When my classes are over. Hopefully the fall. I have a job lined up in Manhattan. I can't wait to start earning some real money again. I feel awfully poor right now."

Julia caught the look her mother shot Aunt Margie. She knew they were both thinking "husband material".

After Steve left, Julia turned to her mother.

"You can't fool me. I know what you and Aunt Margie were doing."

"What do you mean, dear? We weren't doing anything."

"Having that guy suddenly show up while we're eating."

Aunt Margie laughed.

"She's too smart for us, Ruthie."

"Well, what do you think of him, Julia?" Mrs. Jahns said. "Isn't he a nice fellow?"

"Mom, please."

"I have to look out for my daughter. There's no harm in that."

"Thanks, Mom, but if you get too pushy, people are going to know what you're up to."

Hours later, after Julia had boarded her plane, Ruth Jahns turned to her sister.

"What did you think?"

"She didn't seem turned off by him. And did you notice Steve looked over at her quite a bit? I bet he thought she was a cutie. Steve is lonely but Ned said he's not one to just date anybody. And his mother told me he is looking for a nice girl. Twenty-seven is an age most men want to settle down."

"What will be, will be," Mrs. Jahns said with a sigh. "Maybe he'll look her up when he moves back home."

"I'm sure he will. By the way, Ruthie, did you give Julia that strange looking pendant she's been wearing?"

Mrs. Jahns shook her head.

"No, I thought you did."

"No, I didn't. But I'm glad it's not from you because I wanted to say it's the ugliest piece of jewelry I've ever seen."

The two women looked at one another and burst out laughing.

* * *

Aiden Hunter stared at the package in his hand. He was certain the photos of his mother were inside the padded envelope. Guenther had not forgotten to mail them to him after all.

He felt annoyance when he thought of Guenther's advice about Julia. How arrogant he still was, despite trying to play the role of caring sibling. His own marriage ending, how dare he sneer about a possible marriage to Julia.

Aiden placed the unopened parcel on his coffee table and turned on the television. A sense of trepidation beset him. He could not bring himself to unseal the envelope. For so long the only reminder of his mother's face had been captured in that one photograph he kept in his office. Seeing any other likeness of her frightened him.

He picked up the one postcard he had received from Julia. She would soon be returning and he would see her. Another note lay in his bathrobe pocket. He put his hand around it and quickly let go, as if he had been burned.

I love you, please don't ignore me, the note had said. *I love you. I love you. If you leave me, I will kill myself.*

Aiden reached for the bottle he had hidden from Guenther's view.

* * *

Julia arrived home and unpacked her suitcase. She checked on her parakeets. Ned had taken care of them in her absence. They twittered in excitement at the sound of her voice.

"Did you miss me?" she said, putting her hand into the cage. One bird hopped onto her finger.

"I missed you, too."

The parakeet chattered and she looked into its tiny black eyes.

"Aiden's eyes are almost as dark as yours," she said aloud.

The bird cocked its head as if it understood.

"I wonder if Aiden will be as glad to see me as you are. Well, back in the cage you go."

As she piled clothes into the hamper, she thought of her aunt and the blatant matchmaking attempt with Steve Lundquist. It was funny, but while Julia did not feel any interest in Steve with her mind --- why, she didn't know him at all --- her body had felt drawn to him. If he had tried to kiss her at that moment, she would have let him. The thought was a traitorous one for she loved Aiden. Suddenly she felt ashamed and disloyal. It was confusing.

For all her devotion to Aiden Hunter, why had she not ever experienced the rush of heat she had felt when meeting Steve just once?

"Maybe that's what lust is," she said to herself. "Maybe I had a lustful moment. A lustful luncheon!"

She laughed, embarrassed that she was talking to herself.

The phone rang. Alone in the quiet house, Julia jumped in fright. She locked the bird cage door and went into the hallway to pick up the extension.

"Hello?"

"So you are home."

Julia was expecting to hear her mother's voice so the sound of a soft spoken male jarred her. Her heart began pounding.

"Aiden? I can't believe you called me."

"Oh?"

"You've never called me at home."

"Hmmmmmm? I figured you might be there alone."

"I am. How are you? Did you get my postcard?"

"I did."

"I got so sick of Florida. You were right about it being not that great."

"I missed you Saturday."

"I missed you too."

"How have you been?"

"All right. Guenther was here briefly."

"How is he?"

"His charming and delightful self. He had a date with an old flame from Nebraska."

"Really? A date?"

"Yes, I must say, he operates fast. He was always that way. In high school, he had so many friends, fellows and girls."

"Well he is very outgoing."

"So he is."

There was a brief silence.

"So no one is at home with you?"

"No. My cousin picked me up at Newark Airport and dropped me off at home. My family's staying in Florida for another week."

"Would you like me to come by and pick you up?"

"Right now?"

"Yes. What time is it?"

"It's six o'clock."

"Did you eat?"

"No."

"All right then. Why don't I pick you up and we can get something to eat."

"Here in Crane Ridge?"

"Why not?"

Julia was stunned. This was not the Aiden Hunter she knew. Once again, she wondered if he had been drinking.

"Are you okay to drive?"

"Of course. Are you insinuating that I've been drinking? I assure you I'm sober. I will need the directions to your house from the college."

"Okay."

"I'll grab a pen."

"I'm so surprised you want to eat in Crane Ridge. What if someone sees us?"

"So what if they do?

"I don't know, I --- I'm just surprised."

"I surprise myself at times."

"Why don't I just park in the college lot and you can pick me up from there?"

"If you wish."

"That way Ned won't see us."

"Ned?"

"My cousin. If he ever drove by and saw me get into a car with a strange man, he'd immediately call my mother. Or the police."

"Then I shall pick you up in the Raleigh parking lot."

"See you soon."

"I probably will be there by six forty-five."

After hanging up the phone, Julia's hands trembled. Aiden's voice had sounded strange; mysterious. Or was it just her imagination?

It's probably nothing.

Humming, she went into the bathroom to get ready.

* * *

Julia sat in the coffee shop in Crane Ridge across from Aiden, remembering it was where he had first taken her for a meal. Did he realize that it is where they were? She had always heard men were unsentimental and did not cherish such things.

"If any of my students see us together, the tongues will wag," Aiden said. "It's not so odd during the school year but to be seen during the summer like this, well....."

"You always say, who cares what people think."

"Yes, you are right. I don't really care. The only trouble might come from the one biggest gossip on campus. What's her name again, that aging hussy?"

"Mrs. Dee? Sandee?"

"Yes. What an unpleasant mental image."

"She's a gossip all right. You can see why she gets along so well with Laine and Jenny."

"Speaking of which, the habit you finally broke."

"The friendship habit? Yes, even my mother's pleased about that one."

She noticed Aiden was picking at his food.

"Aren't you hungry?"

"Hmmmm, no, I guess not. I have a lot on my mind. So you didn't enjoy Florida?"

"The heat was awful. I couldn't really handle going outside till sundown."

"That sun would have destroyed your fair English skin."

"I am half English you know. And you're pretty white yourself."

"But I don't go to Florida."

"Touché."

Aiden smiled his half-smile.

"And so you came back early. I'm glad."

"What did you do while I was gone?"

"Hmmmm? Not a whole lot. I missed your smiling face. There, you wanted me to say that, didn't you?"

"And your brother came to see you."

"Yes, he did. More to brag about his lady friend than to actually spend time with me."

"So you think he really likes this woman?"

"Knowing Guenther, he'll be married by next year. Easy come, easy go."

"I guess he is just used to being married."

"I suppose so."

Aiden paid their bill and they walked into the summer evening. Julia was happy to be home, happy that she was with an older man who loved her, happy that it was a beautiful evening and all was right with her world. She skipped across the parking lot to the car, Aiden trudging along behind her as he searched for his car keys. He regarded her with amusement.

"My, my, the energy of youth."

"I'm just so glad to be home. The evening is so pretty this time of year, it isn't real hot anymore, and I'm just very happy!"

"I'm glad."

Julia whirled around, flinging her arms outward. She looked up into the sky. The sun had lowered and the colors of pink and blue were breathtaking. Suddenly the world felt soft and romantic. She stood still. Something stirred inside of her, something never before experienced. She felt as if she were growing older at that very moment. The warm air enveloped her body and she turned to Aiden as he went to unlock the car.

"I love you, Aiden."

She spoke the words but they were in a whisper. He did not hear her.

"What did you say?"

Her voice got louder.

"I want to give you a hug."

"Right here? We're in a parking lot."

He got inside the car and she followed, reaching across her seat to hug his neck as he started the engine.

"What has come over you?"

"I don't know."

Aiden pulled out onto the main road, Julia still close to him, her arms around his shoulders.

"If I didn't know you better, I'd say you were imbibing. Or did that tropical sun affect you? You must let go of me or I'm afraid I will run off the road."

She let go of him then, lying back in the seat. He reached for her hand.

"If I sounded strange to you earlier," he said. "I must confess, I am nervous. I wanted to discuss something with you."

"Where are we going?"

"I'm taking you back to your car."

"So what do you want to tell me? Is it something bad?"

"Not at all. I shall tell you as soon as we park."

A few moments later, they were back at Raleigh College. Aiden pulled his car next to where Julia had parked hers.

"I always meant to ask you, Aiden, why don't you move near the college? Why do you live in Tilletsen? It's such a dumpy city."

"There were many reasons why I chose it," Aiden replied. "But if things change in my future, perhaps soon I will not have to live there."

"Is that what you wanted to talk to me about?"

"In a way."

"Before you say anything, I wrote you a poem while I was in Florida."

"You did? Should I be flattered?"

"Yes. I've never written anyone a poem before. I will give it to you but you have to promise not to read it until you're alone."

"All right."

She handed him an envelope.

"It's inside. Now promise you will read it when no one is around."

"That is most of the time. Shall I read it tonight?"

"If you want. Now what is it you wanted to tell me?"

He stuck the envelope into his shirt pocket and turned off the car's engine. All was quiet. No one was around.

"I first want to tell you I missed you very much while you were away."

"I was only gone a few days."

"I know. But I knew you were far away. And I missed you. More than I thought I would. It scared me. I felt like you were going away and never coming back."

"That's so silly! You know I ---"

"Let me continue. It sounds ridiculous to you but it's how I felt. Your absence, though brief, created a terrible emptiness inside myself. I even confessed this to my brother and goodness knows, he's not one I would normally confide in. He thinks you're so very young and this whole thing will die a quiet death."

Julia sat up straight, all her attention now on him. She started to feel nervous.

"I only know how I feel," he said "And I realized I want you here with me all the time. Not just on Saturday."

Julia felt her face redden. She put her hand to her cheek as if to calm the burning.

Again, she felt the out-of-body experience of floating. She was hovering over herself, watching their conversation from above.

What is he going to say? What is he going to say?

"I know you're a young girl, I know I'm in my middle years, but there's something about you that comforts me. When I'm with you, I'm not afraid. I think we would always get along splendidly. I respect you so much, your good morals, your strong beliefs, your --- well, here I am, rattling on, when I really wanted to say --- to ask you ---"

"Aiden?"

"What I need to say to you was….."

He took a deep breath.

"I would like to marry you."

* * *

Julia went to work the following day so preoccupied that a coworker asked if anything were wrong. Every now and then her hands would tremble and she'd drop papers. When her boss asked her for a cup of coffee, she handed him an empty mug.

The scene from the evening before played over in her head. Like a broken tape recorder, she heard the conversation repeat itself.

"Aiden, I'm so shocked at what you just said. I don't know what to tell you."

Looking at his face, his features appeared distorted as if she were viewing a movie with a blurry picture. He did not touch her. His gaze was intent, his eyes darkening as he spoke. He looked at her with deep affection but no passion.

"I'm only nineteen. Marriage to me seems very scary right now. And you know my parents are divorced. I think of that when I think of marriage and I don't think of it often."

Why am I lying? I always thought of marrying!

"It's something out there, in the future. Yet when I do think of it, I do know I want to do it. Someday. I don't want to end up alone my entire life."

What am I trying to say? I don't even know!

"The future comes quickly," Aiden said. "It's here before you can blink."

"I always want us to be together, you know that, but marriage is a big step. And I can't picture you being my husband."

As soon as the words were out, she felt relief.

Husband? Oh my God!

"What do you picture me as then?"

"I don't know."

Aiden her husband? Aiden putting a ring on her finger, *sleeping in bed next to her? Oh my God!*

"You don't realize it now because you're young," Aiden said. "But friendship and love are the strongest things in the world. They are what make for permanent relationships."

What is he saying? He sounds like he is reading from a script! This entire conversation sounds like a bad play!

"You see what marriage based on sex is like: divorce awaits down the road. Sexual passion confuses the mind and it never lasts, despite what the media would have you believe. It's a temporary phenomenon designed to keep the species going. What we have is so much more real."

Oh my God! He's talking about sex! Why is he doing this?

"Please don't say anything more. I have never been with anyone who talked like that. Please stop, it's really embarrassing me."

"I'm sorry. I don't mean to make you uncomfortable."

"I am very uncomfortable."

"I have laid my pride down on the table before you. If anyone should feel uncomfortable, it is I. I have thought about us and I want you with me, living with me, always here."

He paused.

"I see myself one day dying with you beside me."

"That's a depressing thought," Julia said. "I also hope you see yourself dying as a very old man."

"I would be an old man and you would still be a middle-aged person." He smiled. "That seems so strange right now, hmmmm? I cannot picture you my age."

"Neither can I."

"We wouldn't have to live in Tilletsen," he said, talking more to himself than to her. "We could live in Crane Ridge, close to the college. I could support you and you could write. Or plant a garden. Or do whatever you wish. You would probably enjoy writing with no financial strains. Nothing is more ideal than for a creative person to be supported by someone else so they can practice their art. Most people never get that opportunity."

She was silent.

"I can see this has been a shocking revelation."

"I don't know what to say."

"You don't have to say anything. I guess I was saying out loud how I hoped things would be. We have plenty of time. You have plenty of time."

He reached over and touched the pendant around her neck.

"So you like my gift."

"Of course I do. I wear it all the time. I won't take it off. Funny thing is, I actually can't take it off. The clasp is stuck."

"Maybe it's a sign. It will always remain on your neck like I will always remain in your life."

He squeezed her hand, then reached for his glasses which had fallen into his lap.

"Call me tomorrow," he said. "I need to know you're not angry with me."

For the first time, Julia did not want him to touch her hand. His words of devotion did not make her feel loved or protected or cherished. His neediness was annoying.

As she drove home that night, her uneasiness pricked at her heart.

* * *

Aiden Hunter sat in his apartment, shot glass in hand, staring down at the two folded pieces of paper he had placed on the coffee table.

The first was Julia's poem. He picked it up, then put it back down.

The second paper had been left under the door mat. He had read the message earlier but wanted to read it again.

"I love you, Aiden," it began. "I can't go on without you. You've had my heart since that very first time. It's more than sex. The sex is great but it's more than that. I don't know how you feel but I know my heart. I love you and I want to be with you every day, not just when you feel like you have time for me or get the urge."

He filled his glass and took another drink.

"I don't know what I'm going to do if I can't see you. I can't live without knowing there is a chance we will be together forever."

He crumpled the note, tossing it onto the floor.

Julia's poem, on hotel stationery, lay before him.

She wrote me a poem, he thought, but the alcohol was starting to kick in and he felt a dullness creep over his emotions. *I'll read it tomorrow.*

* * *

That first day back at work, Julia winced at what awaited her. Little had been done in her absence; the paperwork in the law office had piled up. After welcoming her back, her boss asked if she could stay late.

"I'm going home for dinner and to watch my kid play ball," Douglas Shaw said at five thirty that evening, picking up his briefcase. "I might try to get back after his game. If you can just get through that one pile of papers, it would be a great help."

"I'll do my best," Julia said, looking up from her typewriter. She must put Aiden's proposal out of her mind if she were to get anything accomplished.

"If you get hungry, there's food in the fridge," Mr. Shaw said. "And plenty of Coca-Colas. I really appreciate your staying."

Soon after her boss left, the phone rang. It was Mary Lou.

"I called your house," Mary Lou said. "You're still at work?"

"Yes, just got back from vacation and I'm under the gun."

"How was Florida? I heard from someone that's where you were."

"Nice but it's good to be home."

"Knowing you, bet you're as white as when you left."

Julia laughed.

"I don't want to keep you," Mary Lou said, "but had to fill you in on the latest gossip."

"Oh no, don't tell me. Now it's Laine who's pregnant!"

"No, but that wouldn't surprise me. I haven't been hanging around the twins that much. They've been going out a lot with Pam."

"How is Pammy?"

"You know her, the little lapdog. She follows the twins around and they treat her like crap."

"She's replaced me as their whipping boy."

"I think so. Anyway, I found out more about Louis Merlowe. Laine and Jenny are friends with Sandee Dee, as you know. I think they've even gone out to eat with her. Laine let something slip the other day. Louis is a homo! And he's in love with someone all right. He's had an affair with this man off and on for several years. Disgusting, isn't it? Picturing a guy with a guy?"

"Ewwww."

"So it's not a woman like we originally thought. It's a man lover. And he is one of the professors. Don't know who; Laine was tight lipped about it."

"A professor?"

"Yes, I'm sure it's the art teacher. He's so queer looking. And he's young, probably near Louis's age."

"I don't think I know him."

"The art teacher's name is Teddy, something like Teddy. Maybe Eddie? I don't remember. Anyway, apparently Louis sits in on classes to hang around the college, just to be near his lover. And the lover has a signal. When he wants to have sex with Louis, he turns on his lamp."

"That's weird."

"Very! Even if it's a bright sunny day, this guy turns on his lamp and that way Louis knows they have a date to meet."

"That is so sick."

"Isn't it? Apparently the affair is over and Louis is sobbing his heart out to his aunt. Typical gay guy, a crybaby."

"Louis seemed so nice."

"I know! And cute too! I just can't get over how someone looking like him could be a homo."

"Wow, that is definitely shocking news."

"Yup. Anyway I'm not hundred percent sure it's the art teacher but I don't know who else it'd be."

"I agree."

"I don't want to keep you, Jules. Just thought I'd fill you in. Have a good night and I'll talk to you soon."

Ugh, Louis and the art professor, how gross!

Julia put the thought out of her mind and went back to work.

* * *

Aiden Hunter stayed in bed late the next morning. He had planned on going to Raleigh to set up his desk for the next semester. As he got up to shower, a call came in from the dean. The campus was closing for the next two days. The air conditioning had gone out and a pipe was leaking. Aiden gratefully returned to his bed. The conversation with Julia had drained his emotions and he felt exhausted. Lying in a fetal position with the sheet over his head, he closed his eyes. The ever-present companions of fear and depression once again threatened to overcome him. He was also hung over. Cursing himself for drinking so much, he willed himself to cheer up. All was not lost. Julia had not accepted his proposal yet she had not rejected it either. The institution of marriage frightened her. Wasn't that to be expected? She was, after all, very young. It was obvious she cared for him. She had cut her vacation short because she had missed him. In time, she would see the light. And she had written him a poem. Though he had not read it, he was sure it spoke of her love. He comforted himself with those thoughts.

At ten o'clock he arose and made himself a cup of tea. The phone rang.

I certainly hope it's not the dean calling back to tell me to come in anyway!

He walked into his bedroom and picked up the extension.

"Yes? Hunter speaking."

"Hello there, Aiden. How are you? Do you remember who this is?"

The male voice sounded familiar but Aiden could not place it.

"No, I'm afraid not."

"Then I guess our evening together wasn't so memorable."

"Who is this?"

"You know who this is."

Aiden paused, his head hazy, trying to remember the voice.

"Think on it a moment and I'll give you some hints. Not so long ago, a summer night, New York City, a hot evening in more ways than one. Maybe two, three martinis. Maybe four, who's counting? Then a ride under the Hudson back to your apartment."

Aiden closed his eyes.

"You're not answering me so I assume you remember. You left your phone number in my --- well, let's say you left me your number."

"I'm sorry. I don't remember."

"I find out your name is Aiden. I think you had told me it was George. No matter."

"I don't know what you're talking about."

"Maybe it was your subconscious acting out."

"As I say, I don't remember. And I'm sorry, I don't know who you are. Please don't call me again. I don't mean to be rude, but my phone number is unlisted for a reason."

"I'm insulted! You have forgotten. You gave me your number. In fact, you said it was the best sex you had ever ---"

"Please stop! This is a mistake. Whoever you are, this whole thing --- well, I'm confused right now. Whatever it was, whatever happened, it was nothing but a mistake. Please don't call me ever again."

Aiden slammed the phone down. Then he unplugged it.

* * *

Julia was so engrossed in her work that she did not notice the time go by. The phone rang and she glanced at the clock. Nine fifteen! No wonder she felt tired. Picking up the receiver, she was relieved to hear her boss's voice.

"I can't believe you're still there," Mr. Shaw said. "Sorry I never made it back. My boy sprained his ankle and we took him to the doctor. I meant to call you earlier but --- you know how it is."

"That's okay. I'm about to leave."

"I can't tell you how much I appreciate your staying. It's late, go on home."

"I am."

"Don't forget to lock up. Thanks again and I don't need you tomorrow till eleven."

Julia shut off the typewriter, covered it and switched off the lights. She took the master key to lock the front door then slipped the key back into the office in the mail slot. The parking lot outside was well lit. Hers was the only car there. Putting her key in the ignition, she expected the motor to hum to life. It didn't. Annoyed, she pressed her foot harder on the pedal, turning the choke. Nothing. She switched on her radio. Nothing. She hit the steering wheel in frustration. Of all times to have a dead battery. Sighing, she looked over at the building next door. An apartment on the second floor had lights on in its windows. Perhaps she could use their phone and call Ned. If he wasn't there, she'd try Mary Lou. If that failed, she'd call Aiden.

She got out of the car, leaving her purse on the seat. Locking all four doors, she began fretting over how she could get the car running by the next day. Ned could no doubt jump-start the battery. But would the battery last? She forgot how much a new one would cost and then felt depressed when she thought of her slim savings account.

As she walked up the stairs to the second floor apartment, she heard loud music emanating from behind the door. At least she would not be waking up an old couple! The doorbell was broken so she knocked.

A disheveled, overweight young man answered the door, his eyes glassy. Dark blond hair, uncombed and unwashed, hung below his collar. His face bore the beginnings of a beard. Opening the door wide at the sight of her, Julia could see three other young men in the room behind him.

Raising her voice over the din, Julia asked to use his phone.

"What?" the young man said, shaking his head.

"I need to use your phone if that's okay. My car won't start."

"Come in, come in."

The young man motioned for his friends to turn down the stereo.

"We have a guest." And to Julia: "This way, please."

The young man bowed, motioning to the kitchen where the telephone hung on the wall.

As Julia walked to the phone, she did not notice the man wink at his friends. Her mind was anxious, hoping Nick would be home to take her call and if not, how she could get her car running. She had just finished dialing when she felt someone grab her arm. Not realizing the connection had been made, the young man let the receiver drop to the floor. He whirled Julia around and to her disbelief and horror, tried to kiss her.

Ned, relaxing at home with his girlfriend Christine and friend Steve Lundquist, picked up after the first ring. He hoped the caller was Julia for he had not been able to reach her. His old buddy Steve had dropped by, surprising him, and the three decided to go out for pizza. Steve had mentioned he had just met Julia and Ned decided to take her along with them. Who knows? Maybe his cousin would like his buddy and a romance would develop. Besides, his Aunt Ruth had asked him to look out for Julia and he felt guilty that he had not been doing so.

As the evening wore on, Christine had mentioned the pizza.

"Are we going to go out or not? How late is Julia working?"

"I don't know but I'm sure she should be home by now," Ned said. He was about to pick up the phone again when it rang.

What happened next made him feel sick. He heard the receiver drop, then a scream. The high-pitched voice sounded like his cousin's but he couldn't be sure.

"Julia? Is that you?"

Steve and Christine stopped their conversation and looked at him.

"What's the matter, honey?" Christine asked.

"Stay on the line, don't hang it up." Ned handed her the receiver.

He grabbed his car keys off the coffee table.

"What's wrong?" Steve asked.

"I have to go. I think it's my cousin."

Steve looked at Christine, whose face had paled.

"I'm going to run by her office first, then her house," Ned said. "I don't know where she is."

"Ned," Christine said, the receiver to her ear, "Whoever it is on the other end is crying and yelling. It's a girl. And I can hear guys laughing."

Steve got to his feet.

"I'm going with you."

The two young men ran out the door into the night.

CHAPTER TEN

Aiden Hunter woke that following day late in the afternoon, forgetting he had turned off his telephone. His head ached and there was a knot in the pit of his stomach. The knot turned into a swarm of raging insects, burning and tormenting him. Trying to get out of bed by swinging his legs over the side, he uttered a groan and fell back onto his pillow. He could not get to his feet. Knowing he had not taken a drink the night before, he wondered if he had food poisoning. But he had eaten at home, consuming only saltines and cheese. *Must be the stomach flu*, he thought, and then everything blurred as nausea overcame him. He had forgotten how wretched one could feel with such an ailment.

After a few hours had passed, his stomach calmed down. Able to walk into the bathroom, he felt well enough to become self-pitying. His thoughts immediately turned to Julia and he wondered why she had not called. It was already seven o'clock in the evening. She had promised to call him. This is when he needed her! He was so sick and no one was around to help him.

I could die here and no one would know!

Where was Guenther? Surely his brother should call him as well! Why did he have to suffer alone?

A more sinister thought came to him. What if Julia never called again?

Maybe the marriage talk scared her away forever.

He returned to his room and reached over to the nightstand where the telephone sat. It was then he noticed it was unplugged.

What an ass I am.

Relief flooded through him. He put the phone back into the jack and left the bedroom to take a shower. He would call Julia as soon as he had freshened up.

* * *

Julia had never been more frightened in all her life. Grabbed by the arm and thrust onto the broad chest of a complete stranger, she screamed, instinctively flailing her one free arm and kicking her legs. Her glasses wobbled as she struggled and she feared they would fall off, leaving her almost blind.

"Leave me alone! Get away from me!"

Her protests were in vain. She was no match for the beefy, two hundred pound male who held onto her, his foul smelling breath moistening the side of her face. She averted her head, her expression one of horror and disgust. Being too intoxicated to notice, the young man held her against him with one arm, the other hand free to push her mouth closer to his. Hearing the men in the apartment laughing in drunken abandon, Julia's heart began to pound in panic.

Oh my God!

"Hey, Richie, I think she likes you," one called out. "She's all red in the face. And she forgot about her phone call!"

The chubby man named Richie, still holding Julia, looked over at his buddy and grinned. His yellow teeth matched the color of his greasy hair. He grabbed Julia around the neck so that her head was forced against his chest. His tee shirt was stained and smelled like beer.

"Hey, man, I think you're right," he said, his voice slurring as he shifted from one foot to the other. "And she's a cute one, huh? I'm gonna give her what she wants."

In the midst of her terror, a strange thought came to Julia. The one time she had seen Aiden drunk, he had never been like this. Never would he try to hurt or frighten her. Alcohol was a strange thing, a friend to those who consumed it, yet an enemy to everyone else.

Richie attempted to kiss her but his clumsy movements and Julia's squirming made him miss and his mouth landed on her forehead. Julia screamed again, this time hollering as loud and as long as her lungs could hold out.

"Come on, baby," he said, releasing his hand from her arm for a moment and wiping his mouth. "Don't be shy. And dammit, keep the bellyaching down a few decibels."

His friends, lounging in the living room and watching the scene unfold before them, howled in delight. Their laughter sounded evil to Julia and far away, as if demon spirits had entered the apartment and were there to torment her.

Richie pinned her arms behind her and walked her over to a settee in the corner of the room.

"Relax, baby, relax. It's party time. We were just having a few beers and a few joints before you came. Now that you're here, it's gonna be even better. Richie ain't gonna hurt you."

He turned to his buddies.

"Ain't that right, fellas? Have I ever hurt a woman?"

His friends all booed.

"Nah, Richie ain't ever hurt a woman. I've hurt plenty of men though. But a woman? Nah, never. Especially one as young as you. You kinda look like the churchy type, like a librarian. Women are for fun, for making love. Now I said, relax. You're gonna have a good time with us. It's party time and you knocking on the door was just what the doctor ordered."

"What you talking about, man?" his one friend said. "This party's been going on for hours now. We're just waiting to the host to show up."

"What host?" another said.

"Yes, but now it's gonna get interesting," another man said. "See if there's another beer in that fridge, C.J. And I want it cold!"

Richie sat down and pulled Julia onto his lap. Holding her tightly against him so she could not get up, he hollered to his friend, "Bring me one too!"

"How about one for the girl?"

"Yeah, good idea. How about it, darlin'? You want a beer? And what's your name by the way?"

"Let me out of here," Julia said. "Keep your filthy hands off me. You're a pig. I want to go home."

With that said, she burst into tears, sobbing until she felt her chest would explode. Though outwardly hysterical, there was a part of her, deep inside, that remained calm and detached. She prayed someone would find her, that nothing bad would happen to her. Her tears continued but she felt strangely comforted.

* * *

As Ned ran to his car, he turned to see Steve not far behind.

"We'll go to her office first," Ned said as he put his keys in the ignition. "Check to see if her car's still there. It's a tan Falcon. Then we'll see if she's in the office. If the car's not there, we'll go to her house. I hope nobody broke in."

"I'm praying," Steve said. He closed his eyes and his lips moved silently.

Ned regarded his friend with a crooked smile.

"Sorry, buddy, I'll sit this one out. I'm not that religious. I don't think God will even know who he's talking to."

Their trip was short as Julia's office was three blocks away. As they pulled into the parking lot, Steve pointed to the car.

"That's it," Ned said. "That's hers. But where is she?"

"Is this her building?"

"Yeah. But Shaw's office is dark. What the hell is going on?"

"Park here. Let's find out."

The two men got out of the vehicle.

"Hey, what's over there," Steve said. "Looks like an apartment in that building next door. The windows are open and a stereo's blasting. Maybe whoever lives there saw something."

"Or maybe that's where she is."

Ned told Steve to check out the apartment while he went up to Julia's office. He wished he could call Christine to find out if Julia had tried to contact them. Maybe the caller had not been Julia after all but someone who had misdialed. He knew if anything happened to his cousin, he would never be able to forgive himself.

Steve ran up the steps to the apartment and banged on the door with his fist. At that moment, he heard a female scream. He pushed against the door with his shoulder and it flung open.

Everything happened so fast after that. Richie, surprised at the unexpected visitor, released Julia and she leaped to her feet, running to Steve. Richie's cohorts ran out the back door and down the fire escape.

"What's going on in here?" Steve said, Julia now in his arms, sobbing. "What are you doing with this girl? I'm calling the police."

Richie staggered across the room.

"Hey, man, keep it cool. Nothing happened. Nothing at all."

"He wouldn't let me go," Julia said. "He held me and wouldn't let me leave. I just knocked on his door to use his phone because my car broke down."

"Calm down," Steve said. "Everything's going to be fine now."

"Now don't go lying to your friend," Richie said to Julia. Then to Steve, "I didn't touch her, man. If you call the cops, it's your word against mine."

"You scumbag," Steve said. "You better believe we'll call the police."

He turned to Julia, his arm around her shoulders.

"Let's get out of here. Ned's with me. He'll be glad you're safe."

Julia could not stop crying. Relief flooded over her yet she still trembled. The moment she had seen Steve come through the door, she felt God had sent an angel. The overhead light had played on his strawberry blond hair, giving him a celestial aura.

His arm still around her shoulders, they walked down the stairs and to the car.

* * *

Aiden's shower done, he sat on his bed and decided to phone Julia. Glancing at the clock, he noticed it was nearly eight. Julia would not be in her office anymore, she would be at home. Should he call her at home? He had forgotten what she had told him about her family returning. As he lifted the receiver, he was interrupted by a knock at his door. Annoyed, he walked through the living room, hoping it weren't some pesky salesman or a religious solicitor. Of late, he had been getting quite a few of them.

He opened the door, prepared to be irritated.

"Yes?"

A pair of piercing blue-green eyes looked into his. At that moment, Aiden forgot about his call to Julia. He did not remember he had proposed marriage to her. His stomach came alive again, but this time it rumbled with excitement, not nausea.

"It's me. I am not leaving you another note. I couldn't stay away."

Aiden opened the door wider. He heard the twittering sound of a pair of birds outside the window. And for the next several hours, Aiden Hunter lost all track of time.

* * *

Julia sat on Ned's couch, surrounded by her cousin and his friends, still trembling. Every now and then, Steve Lundquist would reach over and pat her arm. Her skin still crawled from where Richie had touched her and she shuddered when she thought of what might have happened if Steve had not arrived when he did. Ned brought her a glass of iced tea and asked if he should call her mother.

"I feel guilty about this, Jules."

"No!" Julia said. "Do not call her! She would worry for nothing. She and Aunt Margie are having the time of the lives, this would just ruin their vacation."

"I want to call the cops," Ned said. "We should've called before that jerk got away."

"It wasn't even his apartment," Steve said. "It was vacated and somehow he had a key to get in. We don't even know his last name or where he's from."

"Too bad we don't have telephones you can carry with you," Christine said. "You could have called them while you were still there."

"Should we call the police now?" Ned asked.

"No, Ned, no," Julia said. "I want to forget the whole thing. I don't want them knowing where I live, that my mother's alone, my last name or anything about me. Please, just forget it."

"I understand what she's saying," Christine said. "Sometimes these druggy type people don't even go to jail and he might try to get even."

"It's my fault," Ned said. "I should have known you were working late and I should've driven you home."

"It's nothing you did," Julia said. "It's Crane Ridge. I thought I was safe. I was stupid to knock on anyone's door."

There was a pause.

"Did he hurt you, Jules," Nick said, lowering his voice. "Did he…..?"

"Let me talk to her alone," Christine interrupted. She took Julia's arm and led her into the kitchen.

"Ned's too embarrassed to ask you but he wants to know if the guy did anything sexual in nature."

Julia put her face in her hands.

"He didn't but I felt it was going to lead to that."

"I'm so sorry."

Christine gave her a hug.

"Well, thank God the guys got to you in time."

"I was stupid," Julia said. "I sure learned my lesson."

"Not stupid, just too trusting. I guess no one can let their guard down, not even in a town like this where we're fooled into thinking we're always safe."

They went back into the living room, Christine snuggling next to Ned on the couch, Julia sitting beside Steve on the loveseat.

"I'm okay," Julia said to her cousin.

"God certainly protected you tonight," Steve said, smiling at her. "Who would have thought, after meeting you in Florida, I'd be seeing you again so soon and under such strange circumstances?"

"I want you to stay here for the night, Jules," Ned said. "I don't think you should go home to an empty house."

"No, I'll be fine."

Julia did not want to admit she was not fine. Her hands shook as she sipped her iced tea. She wanted to call Aiden, cry as she told him what had happened and then hear him get angry and comfort her. As she watched Christine with Ned, she suddenly wanted what they both had.

"I want to go home now, Ned."

"Okay, give me a minute."

"I'll drive her home," Steve offered. "That way you and Christine can, uh, stay comfortable."

"Is that okay, Jules?" Ned asked.

Julia nodded.

"I still can't believe what happened," Christine said. "This town never had any problems. But I guess you never know."

"There are transients in every town," Steve said. "And people sometimes never report things."

"This isn't the town it used to be," Ned said, throwing his buddy the car keys. "And Jules, I still say you're better off tonight sleeping in a house with two men. Steve's staying here with me for the next few days."

Julia shook her head.

"I just want to go home."

* * *

Aiden Hunter sat on the couch, his robe bunched around him, a shot glass in his hand. The day had turned dark, like a typical August afternoon with a thunderstorm brewing. The colorless liquid he continually poured down his throat was slowly assuaging his feelings of self-loathing. He stared at the television screen, as if in a trance, neither hearing nor seeing the program.

Little sweat drops formed around his neck. He had forgotten to turn on his air conditioner and the room was becoming hot. Even in his discomfort, he did not get up to turn it on. Someone as despicable as himself did not deserve to be comfortable.

The phone rang and he jumped. In the morgue-like quiet of the apartment, noise was a rude interruption. He thought about ignoring its loud demand, then something made him get to his feet and walk to the bedroom where he picked up the receiver.

"Hello?"

His voice sounded far away, even to his own ears.

"Aiden? Is that you? Are you all right?"

It was his brother. He had half-hoped it would be another male voice, had half-hoped it would not. He didn't know if he should feel relieved or disappointed. The memories of the night before were dimming and his body felt as if it had been abandoned. He took another swallow before answering.

"I'm fine."

"I'm glad, I'm glad. You sound tired," Guenther said. "I hope I didn't wake you. Were you taking a nap?"

"Yes."

"What's the temperature out there? We've hit one hundred today."

"I haven't looked. Must be over ninety."

"Yes, it makes me want the winter back," Guenther chuckled. "And I'm not one for cold weather."

Please stop the small talk, Aiden thought. *Please!*

"I didn't wake you up, did I?"

"No, no, I told you no."

"I just wanted to ask you if you have any free time in the next few weeks."

"What?"

"You have an open invitation to come out and see us. As I told you, my Shelley's getting married next spring and we're throwing her an engagement party the first Friday in September. It would be nice if you could fly out for that."

Aiden's head was foggy. His brother's words sounded far away as if he were on a pier and yelling across the water.

"What did you say?"

Guenther paused.

"Aiden, I said ---"

His voice seemed to get louder now, like he was screaming through a megaphone. Aiden winced. He rubbed his temple with his knuckles. A sharp pain formed around his eyes.

"Aiden, are you all right? Have you been drinking?"

"Please, stop shouting. My head can't stand it."

"Stand what? I'm not shouting. My God, you're drunk, aren't you? It's two o'clock in the afternoon and you're drunk."

"Please, Guenther."

"All right. I don't want to hear it. I'll call you later."

The phone went dead. The pounding in Aiden's head intensified and he laid down on the bed, the phone still in his hand.

* * *

Julia said little to Steve Lundquist on the drive back to her house. He was wise enough to avoid casual conversation. After walking her to the door, he patted her shoulder and turned to leave.

Once inside, Julia flicked on every light she could. Then she filled the bathtub with hot soapy water. As the water rose, she went into the kitchen and dialed Aiden's number. It was nearly midnight but she had to talk to him. To her surprise, the line was busy. She stared at the receiver, not wanting to return it to its cradle, hoping he would somehow magically pick up.

Oh Aiden, why aren't you there?

Burning tears began in the corners of her eyes but she forced them back.

After bathing, she once again tried his number. It was still busy. Now lonely and scared, she burst into tears. No one could hear her, no one was there to calm her down. Though the air was close, she put on her heaviest robe. Searching the back of her closet, she found her old stuffed dog, the one who was missing both ears. Shaking the dust off it, she climbed into bed, burying her face in the pillow, the dog tucked against her side. She brought her knees up and curled into a fetal position. The moon lit a path through her room from an open window and sleep came almost at once.

* * *

Aiden Hunter could not remember a time he had so vivid a dream. He was walking in a field, through flowers of all shapes and colors, but could not recall his destination. Confused, he then found himself on a large bed, the coverlet pulled back, exposing sheets that shone like gold. Bright yellow dandelions were strewn across the pillow. Exhausted, he sunk down into the mattress and the room grew dim. A warm body snuggled against him and loving hands caressed his face. Feeling safe and comforted, he turned toward the figure. But he could not see who it was. He felt soft lips brush against his cheek and he tried to kiss his benefactor as passion rose inside him. He wanted to melt in this lover's embrace. But in the first ray of light, he found himself alone, and he stretched out his arms, desperate to have back an all-consuming lovemaking. It was no use. No one was there. Sorrow ate at him and he realized, with deep despair, that this is how it would always be.

The dream woke Aiden with a start. He looked around, wondering what time it was, what day it was, and why his head felt like lead. He tried to return to a sleep state so he could recapture the dream. *Who was that person?* Why did he have to wake up before he knew?

Thoughts of Julia came to him then and in a panic he wondered how many days had gone by since he had heard from her. He grabbed his alarm clock and squinted to read the face. Six o'clock. Evening or morning? His stomach rumbled with hunger pangs. A vague recollection of hearing from Guenther arose but he wasn't sure if his brother had actually spoken to him or he had just dreamt it. Should he call Guenther back? Deciding to phone Julia first, he realized he needed a drink.

* * *

Julia slept most of the following day. She arose at two in the afternoon and took another bath. Feeling achy, she returned to bed. The phone rang but she ignored it. Ned stopped by later, leaving a note on the kitchen table that Douglas Shaw had contacted him. Her cousin explained to her boss what had happened and that Julia was staying home. Ned later drove to where her car was parked and tried to jump start it. It refused to turn over so he called a tow and had it taken away.

"I'm sorry you won't be able to drive it for a few days, Jules," Ned said in his note. "It's probably a wiring problem. But if you need a lift, let me know. I'm here."

Around four o'clock she decided to call Aiden. To her dismay, his line was still busy.

She phoned Ned.

"You have to do me a big favor. I need to borrow your car."

"Borrow it?"

"Yes, I have something to do, somewhere to go. Please let me use it for just a few hours."

"Sure you can have it, Jules, but why the secrecy. You been seeing someone we don't know about?"

"Don't be silly, Ned. I have something to do. Trust me, it's important."

"Okay, I'll have drop the car off soon. Steve is here and we'll use his rent-a-car for the day."

"Thanks so much!"

"Keep safe this time, will you? I want to give Aunt Ruth a good report on how I did as your protector."

"You're the best, Ned."

* * *

Julia reached Aiden's apartment early in the evening. She was relieved to see his Fiat parked in front. Adrenaline had been building up inside her during her drive and she couldn't wait to throw herself in his arms.

She had made a decision. It was important and it was something she had to tell him in person.

She was going to tell him yes, she would marry him!

She would marry him after all, even though she was just nineteen, even though she hadn't been sure of her feelings for him just a week ago. She wanted to be protected, to feel shielded, to have someone older looking out for her, to feel arms around her when she was scared or uncertain. She wanted to hurry and see him so she could tell him all these things while she still had the courage.

She wanted to sit on the couch next to him, have his arm around her, and this time she would not feel the least bit boxed in or smothered. This time it would feel right, the answer to her prayers and all the dreams she had of wanting an older man's love that had burned in her heart since she was thirteen years old.

She would do it. She would marry Aiden Hunter.

And then the twins would see her married, married to Aiden, a much older man, and they would feel sorry for all the garbage they had shoved in her face all these years. They would whisper to their friends, wow, Julia really found an older man to love her, isn't that something, and she's getting married before any of us! And this man had no previous wife, no children, no baggage to get in the way. His full attention would be on her and her alone!

Why, those twins could have their precious father, she would have Aiden for her own, and he would be better than any father because he was hers forever. Fathers could get remarried and have new wives but a husband was yours alone. Forever.

Then she thought of her mother and aunt. And Ned. What would they think? Her mother would be upset at first, of course, because of Aiden's age. But she would see how happy her daughter was and all her doubts would dissolve and she'd be thrilled, and Aunt Margie, always positive and cheerful, would be happy too. Ned might have a comment or misgiving but then, being in love himself, he'd congratulate her and maybe offer to walk her down the aisle.

Sandee Dee even came to mind and Julia smiled when she thought about Sandee's reaction to the news that Julia had married Aiden Hunter. Sandee would be appalled and then spread rumors that Aiden was a freak of nature, a pervert who enticed a young girl. Eventually her gossiping would catch up with her and she'd cause so much trouble that the president of Raleigh would put her on probation for defaming a professor and his new wife. Then, fearful of becoming an unemployed registrar, she would be forced to apologize to the entire faculty or spend her days collecting welfare checks. Sandee would no longer shoot Julia pitying looks but give her the respect Aiden Hunter's wife deserved.

And Guenther Hunter! Aiden's brother would be happy, happy for his sibling and happy for Julia, too. Because he was a good person, a decent human being, who truly loved Aiden and wanted him to find peace. Guenther would finally persuade Aiden to return to Nebraska for a visit and this time Aiden would go. He'd want to go because he'd have a new bride on his arm and he would show her off to all the nieces and nephews he had not seen for years. And Julia would be Julia Hunter, not Julia Jahns, a new person! The name sounded so natural that she said it over and over, in her car, on the drive to Aiden's apartment.

All these things jumbled together in her mind, her heart beat wildly and her grip tightened on the steering wheel. Her eyes were intent on the highway before her but her mind was in another world. As she turned the corner to Aiden's street, she noticed a storm cloud overhead. A loud clap of thunder interrupted her thoughts like an angry teacher slapping a daydreaming student. The sky changed from soft pinks and blues to angry black and she shivered.

* * *

Aiden let the phone drop to the floor. Julia had not answered.

The glass he had been holding fell with it, spilling clear liquid onto the throw rug by his bed. He got up and stumbled to the living room. He had trouble negotiating the distance between himself and the couch and almost fell to the floor. Pushing the buttons on the television set, he was annoyed that he could not bring it to life. His screen remained stubbornly silent.

Julia was not at home. She had not taken his call. She had obviously forgotten him. He had no recollection of how many days had gone by since he had last seen her, but he was convinced she no longer cared anything about him. In his mind he saw her face but everything was mixed up. Another face blended into hers, a face of someone who had loved him and then left. Someone who had gone away forever despite his screams of torment, his rage and his overwhelming grief of abandonment.

He started to breather heavier; his chest felt tight. Was he dying? Part of his mind was panicked but another part was indifferent.

I hope I die! I hope everyone feels sorry that I'm gone!

He noticed a padded envelope still sitting unopened on his coffee table. Guenther had sent it. Guenther had wanted him to see what was inside.

I especially hope Guenther feels sorry that I'm dead!

He reached for it and slipped to the floor. Trying to stand up, he wobbled and landed on his knees beside it. He attempted to open the tight seal but his fingers did not obey him. Frustrated, he threw the envelope across the room where it landed against the front door. The impact caused the seal to break open and photos flew all over.

Then he heard the thunder. It sounded like a shotgun blast and he winced. He walked to the window to draw the blinds, at the same time peering out and seeing a car slowing down in front of his building.

He walked to the door, his foot sliding on one of the photographs. He reached down to pick it up. A face from long ago smiled up at him, a young woman's familiar eyes looked into his, and he stopped and stared at the picture, his mouth agape. Beside the woman, pressed against her cheek, was the face of a little black-haired boy. The child's forehead was pressed tightly against the woman's, his bangs almost obscuring her one eyebrow, and his small arms were thrown around her neck.

The little boy is me.

Aiden stared at the photo as if hypnotized. Moments later, he heard a knock at the door which jolted him out of his reverie. He let the photo slip back to the floor. Opening the door, he saw the flushed face of a young woman and in his alcohol-induced confusion, he thought he was seeing a ghost. His hands instinctively went up in front of his face and he stepped backward. One heel caught the edge of the rug and he fell.

* * *

Julia could not believe what she was seeing. The door had opened and in happy expectation, she waited for Aiden to express delighted surprise. Instead, his hair tousled, his face ashen, a stranger who looked like Aiden, in sweatpants and an old terrycloth robe, was backing away from her, his hands up defensively. Her smile faded but before she could speak, he fell backward. She grabbed at his arm but missed. He tumbled to the wooden floor, eyes closed, and she cried, "Oh my God!" and knelt next to him.

He lay on his side and moaned. There were about two dozen black and white photographs scattered all over.

"Aiden, what's wrong? What's the matter with you?"

He did not answer or open his eyes.

Oh my God! This is unreal!

She wondered if she should call an ambulance. But as she put her face closer to his, she could smell alcohol and her heart sank.

"Aiden, listen to me. What's wrong with you? Are you drunk? Did you have too much to drink?"

He turned away from her, rolling on his side.

"You might have hurt yourself. Should I call a doctor? I think you're just drunk but I don't know. Can you please answer me? Please!"

He continued to ignore her. No matter how many times she pulled his arm, he did not answer. For the next few minutes, there was nothing she could hear but the rumbling of thunder and the sound of her own voice.

* * *

The storm knocked out the power and Julia remained in Aiden's apartment in darkness for the next hour. She sat on the sofa watching him, not knowing what to do. He remained on the floor, not moving. She was afraid to leave him, scared he might die. Could people expire from too much alcohol? She had heard of a college boy across town who had drank himself to death. His friends had left him alone and he had passed away. What if Aiden stopped breathing? What if he were in a coma, not asleep at all, and he died during the night?

After a while she arose and made sure the front door was locked. She then went into the bedroom, took a pillow off the bed and slipped it under his head. The discarded photographs caught her eye and she bent down to pick them up, stacking them in a pile. One in particular stood out: it was larger than all the others. It was the photo of a young woman and her large eyes seemed to beg for attention. Julia was drawn to the woman's eyes. Although the picture was old, the woman in an antiquated housedress, Julia felt she was seeing a reflection of herself. The photo was black and white but one could see the young woman was fair-complexioned with light colored hair. Her facial features were a replication of Julia's own. Fine, wispy hair was pulled back into a bun and her expression was pensive. Except for the woman having a broader forehead, she could have been Julia's twin. Cradling the photo, Julia recalled the shabby picture she had once seen in Aiden's office. This was the same young woman. This was Ada Hunter, the mother who had died so young, leaving two small boys behind and never knowing the men they had become.

This is Aiden and Guenther's mother!

Julia looked over at Aiden who remained on the floor. She looked at the photograph. Then she walked over to the television set and placed the picture upright against the antenna. The woman's eyes were now facing the man who remained prone, troubled even in sleep.

* * *

Several hours later, Julia left Aiden's apartment.

As she drove back to Crane Ridge, disappointment weighed so heavily on her heart she felt numb. Tears would not come though she wanted to cry.

I feel sick. I want to go home and curl up into a ball and not wake up for a year.

She pulled into Ned's driveway, not even noticing that he and Steve Lundquist were talking together by the garage.

"Hey, Jules, you were sure gone a long time. Everything okay?"

Ned poked his head into the car and grinned.

"Yes," she said, forcing a smile. "Thanks for the car. Can you drive me home?"

"Sure thing. Let me run inside and grab my wallet."

After Ned left, Steve walked over to her.

"How are you?"

"I'm okay."

"I wanted to ask you something. Please don't feel you have to say yes."

Why did those words sound so familiar?

I have the weirdest feeling of déjà vu!

"It's kind of late notice," Steve said. "But I have a wedding to go to this weekend. I'm in need of a date. Would you do me the honor?"

I don't want to go anywhere. Oh, God, please just make everyone disappear. I can't deal with this right now. Please, please let me feel happier. I feel so awful.

Again, she felt disassociated from her body.

And then she heard her voice say, "Yes."

CHAPTER ELEVEN

It was only October, yet snow was beginning to fall when she pulled up in front of Aiden's apartment. The afternoon had turned grey and damp and few cars were on the road. Julia hurried up the sidewalk, tucking her purse under her arm. She wore her old beige coat, the one her friends used to tease her about because it looked ratty. She liked it because it was old and familiar. Her hands balled into fists, she approached Aiden's door and was surprised that he appeared in front of her without her having to knock. His black hair was tousled, his face ashen and dark circles formed half-moons under his eyes.

"The ghost of Christmas past," he said when he saw her.

"More like Halloween," she replied.

"Yes, well it's snowing so it feels like December today."

"May I come in?"

He held the door open.

"I can't believe I'm finally seeing you," he said as she stepped into the living room. "What has it been, six weeks now?"

"I tried calling you. In, fact I've called you over and over. You don't answer the phone."

"A lot has happened."

"That's no excuse for ignoring the phone."

"I have had a very bad time."

"How can anyone reach you if you don't answer a phone?"

"Please, please stop. I'm not at all well."

"I'm sorry, I'm sorry you are not well. But I'm hurt. I'm beyond hurt."

"You are hurt? I am hurt. I am so hurt, you have no idea what your words are doing to me. Do you know what has happened? Have you even asked?"

"I tried to ask. I tried to call."

"I don't remember not answering my phone. I have not heard from you and I figured it was because of --- because of my declaration. Your absence said enough."

"The last time I saw you, you were lying drunk on your floor. I stayed with you for hours and you never woke up. I had to leave. I couldn't stand seeing you like that."

"I don't remember. All I know is, you disappeared."

"Disappeared? It's *you* who have disappeared!"

Aiden sat on the couch, his head in his hands.

"Please, please stop."

Julia took off her coat and sat down on a chair across from him. His apartment, never tidy, looked as if a tornado had hit. Shot glasses littered the coffee table. Books, papers, cups and clothing were strewn across the floor.

"Would you like a cup of tea?" Aiden said.

"No. I just came to talk. I can't stay long. I wanted to make sure you were okay."

Aiden reached for a glass on the end table beside him.

"There is not a lot to talk about. This --- you and I --- will never work. I now know you do not love me and have never loved me. This is just a game to you."

He took a small sip, then reached for her hand. He raised it to his cheek, gently kissing her palm. Julia froze, captivated, yet irritated by his words.

Alcohol! I smell it! How could he!

The sound of swirling wind hitting the window pane startled them both. Aiden turned toward the glass.

"The weather outside has captured my mood."

"I can see you've been drinking," Julia said. "You're making no sense. Accusing me of playing games, at the same time playing a game yourself."

"And what would that be?"

"Telling me I don't love you, I've rejected you, so you have an excuse to be angry and drink."

Aiden did not answer but walked to the window and looked out.

"Strange, there was no mention of a storm on the news," he said. "How odd for it to be snowing this early."

He turned on his television set. A large cobweb stretched across the screen and he brushed it away.

"Don't you despise television?" he said. "Most of it is pure rot. And the commercials are worse. Look at that one, all those fools smiling as if their lives were perfect. Jackasses, all of them."

He turned the television off and reached for a bottle behind a chair.

"I think I will make us a fresh pot of tea. Amuse yourself for a bit with my roommate."

He handed her a bottle of vodka.

"Here is my companion, my most intimate of friends. You once kept me company, remember?"

"I don't want that," Julia said, putting the bottle on the coffee table. "And I don't want any tea."

She shivered. The room was chilly, the apartment dark.

"I guess you know I took a leave of absence," Aiden called from the kitchen. "I'm not going back to school until next semester. If I return at all. Apparently the English department has a vendetta against me and want me gone."

"I had no idea," Julia said. "I didn't go back to school. I have a lot to tell you, too. What happened?"

"It all begins with the delightful Mrs. Dee, or Cee, or whatever her name is. Apparently I was set up. It's a long story but she claimed I'm a raging alcoholic among other things. In fact, calling me an alcoholic was the most flattering thing she said. I had an interview with the president of Raleigh who told me to take a semester off."

"I always knew that woman was trouble. Are they going to fire you?"

"I don't know."

"Well I didn't know you weren't at school because I wasn't there either. Sandee Dee took great joy in informing me I was no longer needed in the work-study program. She insinuated it was your idea."

"That woman is an ass," Aiden said. "I was never even there. So it looks like we were both deceived."

"I decided that very day to quit college. I'm going to the secretarial school in Fullerton next January. I never wanted to be a teacher anyway."

"So we are both gone."

"Yes."

"My tale of woe is not yet over. I was also accused of making a pass at a former student. More than a pass, I was told we had an affair."

"What student?"

"A male student. He had gotten an associate's degree from Raleigh about five years ago and has returned only to make trouble for me. Said while I was his professor, I had coerced him into a sexual relationship. And then the president added that this young man was a friend of my work-study student, Miss Jahns."

Julia closed her eyes.

"Was it Louis Merlowe? I can't believe it."

"You can't believe what? That he was your friend or that he claims I sexually attacked him?"

"No. I mean, yes. I mean, I can't believe he said that about you. He was never my friend, only an acquaintance. The twins even tried to get me to go out with him."

"Then," Aiden continued, "I was told that Ms. Dee claimed I was having a sexual relationship with you and him at the same time. And that I had had sex with him while he was only seventeen and first attending Raleigh."

"You know he's Sandee's nephew?"

Aiden came into the room, holding a cup of tea.

"Nephew?"

"Yes. Can you see what's happening? She hates you! She probably put him up to all of this."

"I can understand them thinking I was having a sexual relationship with you, but this young man, it's just --- well, it's just disgusting."

"I would not let them get away with this, Aiden. You can fight them."

He sighed.

"I'm afraid I do not have any fight left in me."

"If it's a lie, you have to fight it. I know Louis is a homosexual. If he is chasing after you, then accuses you of being the aggressor, he's got to be stopped."

Aiden looked at her and opened his mouth to speak. Then he changed his mind.

"So, in these six weeks, a lot has gone on."

"And in six weeks," Julia said, "you haven't called to tell me a thing."

"I just felt you did not want to see me anymore. I didn't hear from you. And it all started right after the night I had asked you to marry me."

"I *did* see you after you asked me to marry you. I drove to your apartment. You were so drunk you fell on the floor. I stayed by your side for hours. I came to tell you --- well, I was about to say…."

She couldn't finish.

"If I were indeed that drunk, how could I even know you were here?"

"I needed you that night. And you weren't there for me."

"Obviously I was in need myself. So then you proceeded to ignore me?" Julia shook her head.

"I didn't mean to ignore you. I was confused and I was, well, everything was just so mixed up."

Julia got off the couch and walked to where Aiden stood, still holding his tea cup.

"I felt you let me down," she said. "And when I left you that night, I hoped you would seek me out without me having to run back to you. But you didn't. I guess after that night, I was angry."

"So I was not there for you. And that is why you are now not here for me."

"You're wrong. I am always here for you."

"Are you? I can sense something is different."

"I'm here because I care. I wanted to talk to you."

"You have changed."

"No I haven't."

He sat back down on the couch.

"It's not only the six weeks of absence that unsettles me. I feel this whole thing, our relationship, has changed. You feel different, don't you?"

"You're so negative," Julia said. "Nothing has changed. Why can't you just take life day to day? Why do you see the bad in everything?"

"Because I'm realistic. At my age, one doesn't like living day to day. The years ahead don't stretch onward in a long span of time anymore. I feel impending doom."

"Impending doom? What doom? I think you are taking this way too seriously."

"I really don't want to discuss this any longer."

"Well I do. For once, I want to finish this."

"Go on."

"You can't go into the doldrums because problems come up or because I get confused about things," Julia said. "Because there will always be times people who love you disappoint you. I am not flawless and I cannot live up to your expectations."

"I have never expected you to be perfect."

"But you do. People will let other people down. You can't punish yourself when that happens."

"People have always let me down."

"And that's what you expected of me. But you know what? A lot of it is in your own mind. You say you care for me but you really don't. You care for a *perception* of me. Because truly loving is letting go and giving the loved one the benefit of the doubt."

"I have never really trusted anyone."

"Aiden, you first need to love and trust God. Then all other loves will fall into place. God is the only one who will never let you down for He alone is perfect."

"I don't want preaching. Please stop."

"You do it with your brother too."

"Guenther? Let's not bring him into this."

"You have one brother. You have to give him a chance."

"I have a raging headache. I want to lie down."

"I'm sorry, I'll leave if you want."

"No, please don't. That wasn't a hint for you to go. Please stay."

Julia walked over to the window and looked out.

"It's snowing hard now. My car's completely covered."

"A sign from your God. It's too dangerous to drive. Please stay."

"If you want me to."

"I've been so lonely. I thought if you came by again, I would push you away. I would slam the door in your face and take great pleasure in doing so. But now that you're here, I'm starting to feel better. I told you that once. When you're with me, I'm not afraid."

"I'm glad. And I'm glad you didn't slam the door in my face."

She sat next to him on the couch and patted his arm.

"So the drinking didn't take your loneliness away, did it?"

"No."

He sank deeper into the sofa, laying his head on her shoulder.

This is the closest to me physically you've ever been. And there's absolutely nothing romantic about it.

"Only you take the loneliness away," he said, his words slurring. He closed his eyes. "Only you."

She pulled an afghan lying on the arm of the sofa over the two of them.

"It's cold in here," she said.

"I wish we could stay like this forever. Wrapped up in our cocoon. Hiding from the world."

But I don't want to hide from the world. I want to experience life!

She held her tongue. It was too tiring to argue with an intoxicated person.

He wears me out. I feel like taking a nap myself.

Several minutes went by and she realized Aiden had fallen asleep. Or passed out. Either way, she did not want to have him leaning against her. She got up slowly, and he sank into the cushions. She then adjusted the blanket so it covered his body.

Julia looked out the window for a second time and shivered. The snowstorm had intensified. No way would she attempt to drive home in such weather. Glancing at her watch, she noticed it was almost seven o'clock. She decided to phone her mother and tell her she was sleeping over at a friend's. As she dialed, she looked over at Aiden, who was still asleep, his features peaceful.

Aiden Hunter, you are your own worst enemy.

With nowhere else to go and little to do, she turned on the television and curled up in a chair. It was going to be a long night.

* * *

By eleven that evening, Julia decided to go to sleep. She found a sheet in the linen closet and put it over Aiden's bed. Curling up on top of it, she lie in a fetal position, pulling the edges of the bedspread over herself for warmth. As she lay her head on the pillow, she glanced at the ceramic meadowlark sitting on the nightstand.

So that's what he did with it.

She was flattered that he had chosen to keep it.

Then, in the half-lucid moments between consciousness and sleep, Julia dreamed. She saw the bird suddenly come to life. Hovering over her, it lifted its wings and she felt herself and the creature changing places. Flying out the door, it was now free, while Julia sat perched on Aiden's nightstand, frozen for all eternity.

* * *

Julia awoke the next morning feeling stiff. Her body ached and for a few moments, she couldn't remember where she was. Nothing in the bare, stark room held any familiarity. She rubbed her sleep-laden eyes. As she sat up, she noticed the ceramic bird.

Oh, yes. Now I remember.

She was in Aiden's apartment. It has snowed and she had stayed overnight. She was in his room, on his bed.

But where was Aiden?

She reached for her glasses on the nightstand. Without them, she was as blind as a bat.

Ugh, I feel like a mess, she thought, pushing wisps of hair from her face. *I need a shower. I don't even know where the bathroom is.*

She got up and made her way across the room. From the hallway, she could see Aiden, still on the couch. She found the bathroom and went inside.

I should never have stayed here, she thought. *This was a big mistake.*

After showering, Julia went into the living room and looked out the window. The snow had stopped, her car was covered, but the street looked clear.

Aiden was no longer on the couch. She turned to find him in the kitchen, putting the tea kettle on the stove.

"I'm going to leave soon. As soon as I get that mound of snow off my car."

Aiden turned toward her, his face pale, his eyes bloodshot.

"My goodness, whatever has happened?"

"Do you remember anything about yesterday?"

"Please sit down and have some tea before you leave."

"Okay."

He opened the cabinet and reached for the teabags.

"Or do you prefer coffee? I'm afraid I only have instant."

"Tea is fine," she said, sitting down at the table.

"How are you feeling?" Aiden said as he put two cups on the table. "Did you rest well?"

"I'm okay. Do you remember last night?"

"I do. Not that I could recite everything said, but I do."

"It's hard talking to someone who's been drinking."

"I am sober now. I'm sorry you had to see me like that."

The kettle began whistling. Aiden arose and poured them both a cup of tea.

"Now, he said," he said as he sat back down. "We can enjoy our tea together and have a talk."

A ray of sun poked through the kitchen window and landed between them on the table top. From a distance, Julia thought she heard a bird sing.

Is that my imagination? Or is that a bird singing outside in all that snow?

Her thoughts flashed back to that March night seven months earlier when a robin had landed between them. It had happened right before Aiden had told her he cared for her.

Aiden paused, as if hearing the bird.

"I am sober now. My mind feels clear. You must listen to me because this is important. I was lying there on the sofa, half asleep, half awake and in that state, semi-dreaming. I seem to do my best thinking when that happens."

Julia took a sip of tea.

"If I were any kind of man, any kind of decent human being who truly loved you, I would have acted differently. I would never have tolerated not hearing from you all those weeks. I would have gotten into my car, driven to your house and demanded to see you. I would have fought for you. Fought for our relationship. But I did not."

"So you don't really love me, is that it?"

"I failed you. You see, for all of my education and the many years of life experience I possess that you do not, it was you who were the smarter of the two of us. You instinctively knew that my marrying you would be an egregious mistake. I would not make you happy. I would make you miserable. In time, you would grow to despise me. I do love you but not in a way you need to be loved. I've been a selfish monster and only now am I beginning to see myself for what I am."

Julia started to say something, but closed her mouth.

It's true. And I didn't fight to see him.

"You know," he continued, "that deep in your heart, this was never meant to be. Have you ever wanted to kiss me as a lover? Think about it. Have I ever kissed you? And last night, drunk though I was, did I ever attempt to climb into bed next to you and make love?"

Oh no! Please don't say anything more!

"You see? By looking at your face, I know the very thought of me as a lover makes you sick."

There was a long pause.

"I'm sorry to be so blunt, but it must be said. Guenther, bless his wretched heart, tried to make me see all this but I was too stubborn, too anxious to prove him wrong. I was still the fourteen-year-old boy, competing with a younger brother who always got what he desired. I wanted nothing more than to show him that I could not only marry, but have a cute young wife of twenty. How many forty-five year old men can accomplish that? Guenther saw right through it and called it what it was, sheer lunacy."

Julia closed her eyes.

"Do you understand now?" he said. "Do you see what I'm saying?"

She nodded.

"You're a wonderful person. You deserve a happy life. You do not deserve someone like me, someone who's only thought of his own needs, his own pride and who, up till now, could not admit he was ---"

He stopped, unable to go further. He looked beyond her, his dark eyes lost in something she could not share.

"Aiden," she said. "You do love me?"

"Yes," he said. "I do. But not as a lover, not as a husband. But I will always love you."

"And I will always love you."

Her eyes filled with tears. She was sad, yet happy that he loved her.

"I'm so mixed up," she said. "Everything is so confusing."

"I know."

They were both silent, Aiden stirring his tea while Julia looked down into her cup.

"I guess I better get going," she said a few moments later.

"I will help you get that snow off your car," he said. "And please be careful driving home."

As she drove away that morning, she waved at Aiden who waved back. Neither one knew that would be the last time they ever saw each other.

* * *

Several hours after Julia departed, Guenther Hunter phoned. He had not planned on calling his brother that day, but something told him that he should. Guenther rarely ignored his intuition. It took many rings before Aiden picked up. Guenther was about to scold his brother for the delayed response but at the sound of his weary "hello", decided against it.

"Aiden, are you all right?"

"Yes."

"I just called to say hello. I hope you are well."

"I'm all right."

"Good. I guess that's all I wanted to say to you."

"Thank you, Guenther. It was nice of you to call."

Aiden's tone was so kind and gentle, it rendered Guenther momentarily speechless.

"Before you say anything," Aiden continued. "I have just made a decision today and I only hope I can follow it through. I'm not able to go into it further, but please keep me in your thoughts."

"I assure you, I will," Guenther said. "And I will also do more than just think about you, Aiden. I shall pray for you."

CHAPTER TWELVE

He had felt the pain and weakness for so long. His hand stroked the stiff surface of the hospital sheets but he had forgotten where he was. Chills and sweat assailed him simultaneously. He wanted to give up, to embrace the black abyss he sensed coming towards him. Yet he was afraid. So afraid, his mind began to cry out to God to help him, to take away this terror that was worse than the physical pain.

Then he remembered what Julia had told him many years ago.

"Just promise me one thing. That when you're about to die, if you have the time or the chance, please promise me you'll reach out to God. Tell Him you're sorry for your sins. Tell Him you want Him more than anything. You don't have to do it now because your heart isn't in it. But you must do it before you die. And I pray you have the time. I pray you will know when you're about to face eternity. Because nothing else matters if you mess that up."

He cried out, oh God, oh God, have mercy on me!

And then peace flooded through him. The nurse saw him sigh, then smile. His sunken eyes grew bright and he wanted to tell the nurse hovering over him that Julia had been right.

"Julie?" the nurse said. "Are you calling for Julie?"

Then he saw her. Was it his imagination or did it feel like no time had elapsed between this present moment and the days they had sat together in the cornfield.

"Mother!" he cried out, sitting up, startling the doctor who had entered the room.

Guenther arrived at the hospital later that day but it was too late. Walking into the dim room, the doctor met him and shook his head. The nurse put a comforting arm around his shoulder and walked with him into the hallway.

"Are you Mr. Hunter's relative?"

"Yes, I'm his brother."

"He knew you were coming. I'm terribly sorry you didn't get here in time. But he was very serene at the end," she said. "I hope that is of comfort to you. He called out for his mother."

Guenther put his face in his hands and wept. The nurse turned away to give him privacy.

"Well, Aiden," he whispered. "It's been a long time. But I'm finally taking you home to Nebraska."

* * *

The morning Julia read Professor Riggs' e-mail it had rained for three days. Turning on the computer, she glanced out the window and noted how warm it had been for late October. Her children had been back in school for almost two months and she felt lonely and bored. There was only so much housework one could do. Thank heavens for e-mail! Sometimes she felt her computer was her best friend.

Like most people, Julia Jahns Lundquist was a very different person than she had been at nineteen. After that snowy October day in 1975, she had not seen or heard from Aiden Hunter again. The rest of that year, and the months immediately following, became the soft blur of a distant memory. Life went on and with it came many unexpected surprises, one of them in the person of Julia's father. Wes Jahns popped back up into Julia's life and for a few years they corresponded through the mail. Wes lived long enough to make peace with his family, then passed away shortly before Julia's wedding.

Ruth Jahns and her sister moved to Florida soon after Julia's marriage, sharing a condominium near the ocean. They had waited until Julia was Mrs. Steven Lundquist before departing their home state forever. Four babies made their appearance in the Lundquist home, one after the other. Steve's accounting business, much to their relief, had done well after a shaky start. He volunteered as a youth pastor for their Baptist Church while Julia taught Sunday school. Never had she been happier. The years flew by and before she knew it, her children had reached their teens. With less to do around the house, Steve persuaded his wife to finish college and get her degree. Needing transcripts of her earlier college years, Julia decided to e-mail one of the professors who still taught at Raleigh College. Thomas Riggs, now almost sixty, came to mind. She then promptly forgot she had e-mailed him, until the rainy October morning when she received his reply.

"Hello, Mrs. Lundquist," the message read. "Thank you for your patience regarding the transcripts. You should be getting them shortly. Just to refresh my memory, weren't you the work-study student I knew from years back? You worked for the late Dr. Aiden Hunter, my former colleague. Just to let you know, Aiden Hunter died many years ago. I don't know if you are aware of it. He had AIDS."

Julia read Riggs' e-mail and felt tears in her eyes. Everything came back.

"Yes, I used to work for Dr. Hunter as a work-study student," she wrote back. "But I remember reading of Aiden's death. He could not have had AIDS. I read the obituary. It said he died in December of 1990. And I remember the article saying 'Professor Aiden Hunter, aged sixty, died of cancer.' I had young children at the time and I normally never read the obituaries because I was always so busy. But that day, for some reason, I did."

Professor Riggs' second e-mail came later that day.

"I don't mean to offend you," he said. "But Aiden died of AIDS. His partner passed away from the same disease the following year. Aiden's companion was an associate of mine, Professor Jon Hughes. Surprisingly, they were both originally from Nebraska."

Julia stared at the computer screen, a pain spreading into her chest. For a moment she thought she might be having a heart attack.

Oh Aiden! Aiden!

Alone in her house, she burst into tears.

* * *

In March of 2003, Julia took a plane to Nebraska. The flight was expensive and she did not like flying, but she felt she had to go. Map in hand, she called for a taxi outside the airport in Lincoln. She directed the driver to a quiet spot near a highway where dandelions dotted a lonely meadow. Asking the cabbie to stop, she left the vehicle for a few moments while he patiently waited.

They made the remaining two-mile trip in a matter of minutes. Julia asked the driver once again if he would stop and wait for her. Stepping out of the cab, she glanced at her map to make sure she was taking the right path. Outside a grassy knoll stood an archway. She looked up to see the letters "Fairview" carved in the wood.

Five minutes passed before she found the headstone. Kneeling on the ground, Julia gazed in silence at the inscription. "Aiden Hunter, 1930-1990".

Beside it stood another headstone, much older, cracked and forlorn, "Ada Millicent Hunter, 1911-1936".

Below both names was the etching of a meadowlark.

Julia brushed her fingers against the outline then placed the dandelions she had picked in the meadow in front of both stones.

Reaching into her pocket, she pulled out the dandelion pendant, hidden away for years in her cedar chest, yet retrieved for this journey. She kissed it and placed it back in her pocket.

"I'll never forget you, Aiden," she said aloud. "I loved you. I hope you finally found peace."

She rose to her feet and walked slowly back to the cab, her hair caressed by the cold Nebraskan wind.

EPILOGUE

Julia's poem to Aiden Hunter:

I love you
Let May flow with December, I care not
I've adored you
Since the day your darkened eyes floated over seas of young faces
And from your lips flowed charming melodies of thought

Since I've met you,
Pain goes with me,
Every thought is you and every heartbeat yours alone

Though our ages go not together
Yet if Fate could bind us
I would love you always

Yet if my love, unreturned, melts
With Reality near,

I won't forget you.
Never.
Not tomorrow nor in a million years.

Edwards Brothers Inc.
Ann Arbor MI. USA
May 4, 2018